The Ada Poems

The Watercourse

Fire Lyric

The Swordfish Tooth

FOR CHILDREN

Albert, the Dog Who Liked to Ride in Taxis

Saints Among the Animals

Wallace Hoskins, the Boy Who Grew Down

What Do You See When You Shut Your Eyes?

Rose and Sebastian

An Enlarged Heart

An Enlarged Heart

A PERSONAL HISTORY

Cynthia Zarin

ALFRED A. KNOPF · *New York* · 2013

A number of the chapters contained in this book were previously published, in somewhat different form, in the following publications: "Two Pictures" in *Document;* "Restaurants" (originally titled "When It's Time to Go Out to Dinner") in *Gourmet* and *Granta* online; "Mr. Ferri and the Furrier" in *Little Star Mobile;* "September" (originally titled "Evensong") in *The New York Times;* "Curious Yellow," "Curtains," and "Sperlonga" (originally titled "Earrings") in *The New York Times Magazine;* portions of "Sperlonga" (as "Big Cheese") also appeared in *The New Yorker;* "An Enlarged Heart" in *The New Yorker* and in *The Best American Essays, 2004* edited by Louis Menand (New York: Houghton Mifflin Harcourt, 2004); and "Real Estate" in *Subtropics.*

Grateful acknowledgment is made to the following for permission to reprint previously published material:

Farrar, Straus and Giroux, LLC: Excerpt from "Questions of Travel" from *Poems* by Elizabeth Bishop. Copyright © 2011 by The Alice H. Methfessel Trust. Publisher's note and compilation copyright © 2011 by Farrar, Straus and Giroux, LLC. Reprinted by permission of Farrar, Straus and Giroux, LLC.

This is a work of recollection. Some episodes and sequences of events may have been altered, and some names have been changed.

Library of Congress Cataloging-in-Publication Data

Zarin, Cynthia.
An enlarged heart : a personal history / by Cynthia Zarin. —1st ed.
p. cm.
"This is a Borzoi book."
ISBN 978-1-4000-4271-5 (hardcover)
1. Zarin, Cynthia.   2. Women poets, American—Biography.   3. Poets, American—New York (State)—New York—Biography.   I. Title.
PS3576.A69Z46   2013
811'.54—dc23
[B]   2012036687

Jacket image: *Brisk Day 1,* 1990 by Alex Katz © Alex Katz / Licensed by VAGA, New York, NY
Jacket design by Linda Huang

Manufactured in the United States of America

First Edition

ה

For Eve

and

for Bill

Continent, city, country, society:
the choice is never wide and never free.
And here, or there . . . No. Should we have stayed at home,
wherever that may be?

— ELIZABETH BISHOP,
"Questions of Travel"

Contents

An Enlarged Heart

apartment she had discovered that her husband was having an affair with a younger woman. Now less than a year later, they were divorced. When I first met this woman, whom I will call Joan, I felt I already knew her, because she so reminded me of the mother of a boy I had once loved. She had her long, wide, flat bones and straight brown hair that fell in a comma over her forehead. Both of them were from the South, and decisive. After I had left school, and my friend and I had parted, his mother came once to visit me in the small grimy city where I was bored and unhappy. She was on her way back to India, where for half the year she sat at low wooden tables in houses that flooded during the rainy season and taught women to read. The other half of the year she lived in an apartment in New York near Carl Schurz Park. At that time her life greatly appealed to me, and I imagined that someday I too would do good work, crouching in mud, and bestowing beneficence. I had no idea that I was entirely unsuited to selflessness. As a way out of my boredom and unhappiness and the slight fear I felt every time I walked out the door in this city (once on the way home from a store a car had followed me), I was learning to cook. I had picked up a paperback in a used-book store. It was Elizabeth David's *French Provincial Cooking.* Standing in the bookstore, I'd read, in the section on sweets, the words, "Everyone knows the recipe for chocolate mousse." I did not, but I wanted to. I wanted to be a person who knew things, and I believed then that there was a programmatic way to do this. I was in this city, accompanied by a boyfriend with whom my exchanges had become increasingly rancorous, because I had been given a fellowship to spend a year writing poems, but month after month, I couldn't think of a single poem. Out the back windows of the apartment I could see the blank windows of closed-down redbrick factories, and the huge hands of the electric company clock. The hands of the clock were lit day and night, and folded and unfolded like a giant's pocketknife. I had counted the recipes in the book; if I made one recipe a day, the year would be over. By then, I was sure, I would know what to do next.

The day my friend's mother arrived, I was making onion soup. It was the kind of recipe I liked then, because it took hours. She took the onion out of my hand. I was cutting it the wrong way. She put a second onion on the chopping board and showed me how to make tiny crosshatched squares without splitting the root. "See," she said, "now you know how to cut an onion." The gray sky of the city out the back window of the kitchen was punctuated with white church steeples. Each set of bells was timed differently, so that the five minutes before and after each hour were cacophony. My friend's mother was upset by this. She was drinking whiskey and she put down her glass. The disorganization struck her as unconscionable. Years later I had a friend whose mother threatened to blow up her house if she didn't get a clock that worked, and I thought of those bells.

We had sold the apartment to Joan sight unseen. An acquaintance at the children's school was a friend of Joan and her husband. They wanted to move. They lived in Battery Park City, and it was too close to Ground Zero. Joan was having recurring dreams.

It was her husband who came to see the apartment. He was an actor. He liked everything about it. He walked down the long hall and exclaimed over the view and the steeple. He admired the way my blackened pots and pans hung in rows on the scuffed kitchen wall. I had bought two dozen red lilies and put them in a blue bowl on the table in the living room, and he exclaimed over the lilies.

The subject of money came up. We told him the price of the apartment, which we had thought and talked about endlessly, before his arrival. It seemed preposterous to us that we should own something so valuable. It was as if a sandwich forgotten about for many years at the bottom of an old suitcase filled with sand and the broken-off arm of a starfish, had turned into a tiara.

The purchase of the apartment in the first place had come about almost by accident. I was married then for the first time, and my first husband and I were living on West End Avenue, in a brownstone building. Instead of caring for the brownstone, years before the owner had painted over it, using paint the color of face powder, but swaths of the paint had peeled and fallen off, so that the house was strangely pigmented, like a pinto pony.

The owner was a small, stooped gray man. He required that I make an appearance at his Midtown office, where his name was affixed in peel-off gold letters on a frosted glass door, each time I renewed the lease. Because he was not inclined to spend money on the building, walking in the common front door one was plunged into smells and gloom.

The smells were not entirely his fault. The brownstone was four stories high, and the first and third floors had been cut in half, with one apartment fronting the avenue and the other in back. On the first floor, adjacent to the entrance, lived Marina, a junkie whose complicated life meant that she often forgot to throw out her garbage. In the back apartment a small crouched woman whom I saw, in the years I lived there, leave the house only once, surrounded herself with old newspapers and combustible fabrics. Occasionally, she would have a visitor, who arrived with a plastic bag reeking of curry. Marina ate only sweets, and when she did take out her trash, some of it would fall in the little hall, and tiny roaches would edge the leavings of sugar icing.

On the second floor, every night, a couple with a little boy railed at each other. "You cunt-pig," he shouted at her. "Snake cocksucker!" she lobbed back, as if in another life they had been zoologists and had fallen back down the evolutionary chain, phylum by phylum, until what came up through the grate in the floor was the sound of thwacks and her mewling cries. The very top of the building was inhabited, on and off, by a man who, when I first moved in, told me that he worked in television. He was rarely at home, but when he surfaced, usually in the spring, he spent all day pounding a punching bag he had screwed onto a post on the roof. *Bang, bang, bang,* went the ceiling in my tiny kitchen, rattling the dishes.

I lived on the third floor. In front lived a girl about my age with gingery hair who worked for a publishing company. I had a partially furnished, two-room apartment, the size of a boot box, in the back. One evening I bumped into her in the tiny stairwell, and she was with a boy with whom I had gone to school. He had occasionally contributed small odd essays to the college literary magazine. There was a dispute among our group of friends, which had not been resolved, as to whether he was immensely talented or very stupid, and he had a reputation for dramatic, antisocial gestures (he had once put out a cigarette on his own or someone else's arm, he drank other people's drinks at parties), but he always had plenty of money, so his company was tolerated and even welcomed. If we had met elsewhere, the girl across the hall and I might have become friends—here, however, we guarded against intimacy and exchanged only pleasantries: anything more would have required us to acknowledge the sordid life of the building and how it sank into our dreams. Once, she knocked on the door and asked if I smelled gas.

I had lived intermittently in the apartment for eight years. That flat itself had been a bit of luck. I had sublet it from Adela, a friend of one of my aunts, who was going to Southeast Asia for a year. She came back only once, one rainy afternoon, when she turned up with the man she was going to marry. Screeching, she excoriated me for a stain on her pink satin comforter, a chip on her Indonesian table, and the loss—she counted them—of three spoons. In the end, she left everything behind as worthless, the implication being that I had contaminated her belongings. Just last week, planting marigolds in a pottery jar, in the backyard of the house where we live now, while a few feet away my youngest daughter added on to the hut she was building for her worms with a piece of broken brick, I realized the planter had been Adela's.

I inherited the apartment. Even for that time the rent was incredibly cheap. Soot fell from the skylight into the bathroom. When I was bored or disenchanted I would sit by the Dutch door that opened onto the terrace and peel off the flaking paint with my finger. Over time I discovered, three layers down, hand-painted wallpaper, a pattern of silver chrysanthe-mums on an indigo ground.

On the terrace, I had a few rose bushes in pots. Directly across the alley, the apartment faced a brick wall. To the south, across a drop of four floors, was an identical terrace, which backed up to the corner building, which was planted each year by a Welsh biologist who was the fifth daughter, she once told me, of a fifth daughter. In spring her morning glories turned the old brick blue. To the left, if I leaned out against the para-pet, I could see a few weedy gardens four floors below. One windy day, when I was out, I left an umbrella open. The wind lifted it out of its ramshackle stand, which I had weighted down with an inadequate amount of sand, and it flew a few houses north before dropping into the farthest garden, where it was just visible, pole up, forlorn, in the lower branches of a dogwood. It did not occur to me to abandon it. At the house that belonged to the garden I rang the likeliest buzzer. Time elapsed. It was cold. I had run downstairs without my coat, clutching my latch key. Presently the door, which led to a common hallway in no better shape than my own, was opened by a disheveled man wearing an ornate red velvet dressing gown tied with a black cord. He was naked underneath the robe. "I believe my umbrella is in your backyard," I said. He narrowed his eyes. "Who the hell are you?" he replied. "Mary Poppins?"

He disappeared for some minutes into the long funnel of the house, and returned with the umbrella. Inside the little hall it seemed immense, a gigantic Venus flytrap, its steel corset exposed. In the moment he handed it over something complicit passed between us, a shudder. To me he seemed immensely old. He was perhaps forty.

After that, although I looked out for him in the street, I never saw him again. He certainly did not say hello to me. It may have been he was unrecognizable, out of his fabulous dressing gown, and that minus the umbrella, I was just another girl skittering up the avenue, with my one grocery bag holding fruit, milk, a bottle of wine, and chicken to roast in the tiny kitchen. I also learned later that the couple who would become for a time my greatest friends in those years lived directly across the street. Their son was born there. But at that time I never met them or, if I saw them in the street, it meant nothing to me.

I lived in that apartment like a crab in a shell. Whenever I felt more suspended than usual, I would scuttle off and leave it to friends. Returning, I'd find bits of odd cutlery and linens mixed in with mine; one old friend told me recently that he had fallen in love with the woman who has been his wife for twenty years in that apartment, when he stayed there one summer while I was away. I'd forgotten entirely I'd left the keys for him. Twice while I lived there the apartment was burgled. The first time I found the window open, huge dusty footprints on the windowsill, three floors above the ground, and the ancient tiny television gone; the second time the thief, disregarding the front door, punched a fist-size hole in the wall, reached in, turned the bolt lock, and took a pair of blue satin Ferragamo evening shoes.

In those days I was constantly in love. In my own mind I had been a romantic child (in truth I had been truculent and ungainly), but by now I was hapless. Since arriving in

New York I had been in thrall to a boy I had known in college, who drank too much gin and rolled his own cigarettes using Bambú papers. He longed for pine forests and favored trench coats worn open in the style of Inspector Clouseau. He betrayed me at every turn, and then came back, his arms full of lilacs. When I could no longer bear to live with him, I would let him stay in the flat and I would go elsewhere. One of those times I moved a few blocks away and lived with the mother of a friend in a huge apartment on Riverside Drive; her husband had just left her for a woman who called him by pet names. One of these was "Ducks." I had left with no luggage in the middle of the night. I stayed there for three months, washing the clothes I had worn when I arrived and wearing what I could find in the bureau drawers that had been left behind by her daughters when they went to college. Another time I moved across town to an empty apartment belonging to elderly friends which had just been painted, and was so at a loss that I spent weeks there without once opening the windows, scuffling among their worn chairs and old books signed by dead authors, as if traveling through time by crossing the park, I had catapulted to the end of my own life.

After a time life became more ordinary. Although my husband had been content on his own to live with a hot plate and a bedroll, he attacked the apartment. The layers of paint and paper came down. The walls were now the smooth color of an eggshell. The tiny kitchen with its leaking icebox vanished. Over the shiny new sink a Rube Goldberg contraption funneled the water from drying dishes directly into the drain. I knew now how to make chocolate mousse. In a space no wider than an arm span, I produced turkey galantine, *oeufs mollets,* a tarte tatin. The pitted floor was painted turquoise blue, and the Dutch door where I had sat absentmindedly chipping paint with my fingernail was replaced with one fretted with ironwork, made of tempered glass. Except for the bed, which could only fit in the bedroom sideways, the only place to sit down was a low sofa which had turned up, its walnut frame in pieces, in a friend's barn. I had covered it, impracticably, in ivory silk twill overlaid with green stripes and flowers, the choice of a person who has not yet encountered family life. Much later, when I married again, my second husband conceived an extraordinary disdain for this sofa. It annoys him that it is a late Victorian copy of an early-nineteenth-century design. It sits now in the corner of the dining room of the house, by the long windows, where it was carried four Christmas Eves ago, at my insistence, so there would be a place where we could sit to look at the tree. The upholstery, with the exception of the back, which has held up, is in tatters, made somewhat worse by my attempt to recover it myself in fawn-colored velvet, which is now, in its turn, stained by cats, ground-in Easter candy, and spilled wine, and piled with stacks of tax returns and unread issues of *Maine Antique Digest,* the pages filled with grainy photographs of Shaker cabinets and old weathervanes. At some point the sofa acquired a confederate in a chair, which friends had given me when they left New York for New Mexico, and which I meant to cover in matching twill. There was not enough, and the chair back, once a clear strong pink with yellow starbursts from a second leftover bolt, is now the color of a faded strawberry stain and the starbursts have dimmed. Last week I moved it upstairs to the bedroom, where for the time being it sits like a guest, unencumbered, because we have not yet taken its presence enough for granted to drop laundry and newspapers on it as we pass.

When it became clear that my first husband and I could not spend the rest of our days in the tiny apartment, I began, in a desultory way, reading the classified section of the newspaper. I wanted to move at that time because I wanted to have a baby. The apartment was up four narrow flights of stairs, past Marina and the screamers. It was clearly impossible that we would ever find anything that we could afford, but the reading itself was not unpleasant. One advertisement read: six rooms on park, French windows, secure building, rent or buy. I went to see it. It was next to a dangerous park. To get there, I walked down a deserted street, a street that is not in the least deserted now. There were many things wrong with this apartment. A lurid mural in the long hallway had been inadequately whitewashed, and loose wires snaked along the baseboard. Plaster from the bathroom ceiling filled the tub, and water was leaking out of the refrigerator onto the kitchen floor. Before the owners, who had lived in the apartment only three years, had taken possession, the apartment had been lived in for four decades by three deaf sisters, and above each door was a light bulb, which flashed if the doorbell rang. The owners had punched a hole from the kitchen into the living room, so that standing in the kitchen you could see the view, but the work had not been finished and little mounds of crumpled wallboard had settled on the counter. In order to punch this hole, they had destroyed the original kitchen cabinetry and put up plank shelving to replace it. The back bedroom, which received hardly any light, was painted dark blue. The three rooms that faced the park and the view had been painted pink, yellow, and pale green by hand, by the woman who now owned the apartment. She and her husband, M———, had separated. He was a stonemason, and it was to him that the apartment owed its deep green marble counters and the columns in the living room. The casement French doors opened onto the view and the church steeple. Both were the color of oxidized copper. Beyond the door was a wrought-iron balcony, big enough for flower boxes. The doors closed with an old-fashioned latch and the handle had been touched so often that the brass glowed. It was shaped like an egg, and cool in my hand. I fell in love with the latch and the view.

I called my husband and told him I had found an apartment. It turned out that now the apartment could not be rented, the owner wanted only to sell it. I discussed the previous owner's follies with the broker: the whitewash, the cost of stripping the pink, yellow, and green impasto. Secretly I loved the sunset-colored rooms and could not have cared less about the whitewash. I was in love with the brass handle, and the lobby of the building, which had a white-and-black terrazzo floor, and which I associated in my mind with paintings of Dutch interiors. The price came down a little. Her lawyer, it turned out, had gone to high school with a friend. The price came down a little more. On the day we moved, the movers were eight hours late.

When we moved into the new apartment we were childless. If one of us played the radio down the hall the other could not hear it; after the old place this seemed miraculous, but in the years that followed the silence wore off, because after

I had a child there was nothing in my house that I did not listen for, and my hearing became like that of a fox in a forest, pricked by every rustle in the leaves. In the decade I lived in the apartment my elder daughter was born, and a little while after that her father no longer lived with us. A very tall college girl who looked like Alice in Wonderland came to take care of her while I worked. That same year a woman who lived on the courtyard of the building went mad and, wearing nothing at all, screamed epithets out the window.

The apartment became crowded. There were now three children—my daughter, and my second husband's son and daughter, my stepchildren—and two cats, who demolished the low sofa. We inherited my grandmother's grand piano. Because I was so often up in the night, even now I could find my way in the dark in that apartment. It had an old parquet floor. One child sleepwalked. At night when it was warm, we kept the French doors wide open until we discovered this. As if nothing had happened, my daughter's father began to come back and occasionally sit at the table. The children ate pasta with tomato sauce and chocolate pudding and cinnamon toast. When the baby was born she slept in our room and then moved into the children's room, and her eldest sister moved out and slept next to the piano. There was a tiny television near the piano, and the children sat on the narrow, spoiled sofa and watched films, Fred Astaire in *Top Hat,* or Yul Brynner in *The King and I.* They were mad for these films and would have watched them every night if we had let them. They are still engrossed in films, but later they simply rented any kind of movie imaginable, and watched them on a large screen in the basement of the house where we live now, on a couch we found on the street and lugged home in the rain, and half the time we pretended we didn't know what they were watching, and half the time we swooped down on them and forbade them from watching whatever happened to be on, in the spirit of keeping the upper hand.

Near the end of our tenure in the apartment the brass knob on the French doors started to come off in my hand. At first it was easy to put back on, but after a while it was clear that the doors themselves would have to be replaced. We each knew, secretly, this would not happen. After all, we had fixed nothing in the apartment. From the time I had first moved in, in another life, the apartment had stayed as it was—the plank shelves in the kitchen, the peeling paint, the sunset-colored walls in the living room. When we decided to move it was because one morning there were so many people in the long cramped hall trying to find coats and boots and book bags that it was impossible for anyone to leave, and so it came to us that we would have to leave forever.

When we did, we moved into a house that for years our gaze had fallen on unknowingly, standing below us in the view, a few blocks north of the church. It had been derelict before we bought it, and we lived like vagabonds in its rebuilt rooms and staircases. The puckered surfaces of my grandmother's piano settled next to the stairs. When that night Joan came in her violet coat we sat on the low sofa, whose embroidery had been picked out now entirely by cats and bored children, and she told me what she knew, that her troubles had come from the apartment—she was now going to take down its walls and the long hall, because according to Chinese principles, when you opened the door of the apartment, love flew down the hall and out the window, into the view of the tree and tall green church steeple. She did not hold it against me, or if she did she did not say so, that her husband was the third man named M—— whose marriage had broken up in that apartment in fifteen years, which, we agreed, was peculiar.

When we first acquire what will become our memories, we do not recognize them or know how and when we will go back to them or what they will mean. When we moved to this house we thought for a moment that we would live here forever, but because we are older the years fold and spill. One still morning I was reading at my desk and the door to a closet suddenly shut and then opened again, like a dreamer exhaling. Eventually I will have the despised sofa recovered. By then we will be elsewhere.

Sperlonga

The first time we went to Sperlonga it was by accident. We were in Rome. The plan was to stay there for a week or so, and then travel north, by car. We would stop at Siena, see the pictures by Piero della Francesca in Arezzo, Montalcino, and Borgo San Sepolcro, and then drive to Assisi. I had an old friend who was living in the hills above Assisi in an old schoolhouse. I thought we would visit her. I was then just married for the first time. We had been married for five days when we left Rome for Sperlonga.

In Rome, my husband and I had taken a taxi for what then seemed like an obscene amount of money (lira then were a spendthrift's dream; spending millions and millions for a train ride, we were rich as Croesus, or Onassis, as we would have said in those days). The taxi deposited us in a section west of the center, which consisted of tall, flat apartment buildings that had been constructed along Fascist lines in the 1960s, when Rome expanded after the war. The apartment belonged to a woman called Ivetta. Ivetta had been my brother's Italian teacher. She had short gray hair, dressed in black, chain-smoked, and had the face of a Roman senator. One eye was a dreamy blue-green, the other brown. Her eyes were so different that the shadows her lids and brows cast over them were singular—her right blue eye seemed capable of tenderness while the brown was not. In the beginning, when my brother had written to Ivetta to ask whether we might stay in the apartment while she was away, the understanding he received in return was that during the week of our visit to Rome she would be in Sperlonga, where she had a house, and where she spent most of the summer and many weekends in the spring and the fall. She offered us the apartment, and sent us, via my brother, a telephone number in Sperlonga should we need to contact her. She added that she would apprise the concierge, who had a flat on the *secondo piano, storia,* of our arrival and give him a set of keys that he would give to us.

But when we arrived in the taxi, a Fiat, and were deposited on the sidewalk in front of the building, he was not there. I had the envelope from my brother in my pocket and I carefully scrutinized the address and the building number. Traveling has always made me nervous, and until quite recently new places have frightened me: I live in a house which is four blocks from where I was born, and except for some years of my childhood and when I was away at school, I have always lived within a mile of where I am now. It has always been important to me to be able to visualize where I will be. When I had imagined the week my husband and I would spend in Rome I'd pictured a narrow window set in a deep casement, and a tub of geraniums on the sill.

But the building was tall, forbidding, flat faced. The taxi disappeared, snorting. It had smelled of coffee and cigarette smoke and the smell of the smoke lingered in my hair, in the cool morning. I hadn't slept at all on the airplane and I could feel the pockets of sleep in my joints. It was May. Above the flat roofs of the apartment buildings the sky was full of wind-tossed clouds. The building was entered through large plate-glass doors with metal frames, and we carried our bags through the doors and put them on the floor of the lobby. The floor was made of green marble, set in squares. My husband buzzed the concierge's apartment: the label on the mailbox, into which a buzzer was inserted, like a blind eye, said "Testa." My then-husband's father's family is Italian. His last name is Italian, as is our daughter's. When he is in Italy, although he knows very little of the language and was brought up entirely in a neighborhood of peeling three-story houses in a New England town that has, in the way of so many towns, become and stayed derelict, when he is in Italy, he becomes progressively more Italian. His gestures become broader. While he will not step inside a church when we are home, in Italy he makes excuses to walk into every church in every small town, and when he is there he always dips his fingers in holy water.

But this was our first time together in Italy, and all of this was to come. That morning his response was to hold the buzzer on the concierge's mailbox for longer and longer intervals, until the lobby filled with buzzing. It was like being inside a hive. A few years later, when we were looking for a place to live, we found a house in a field that I loved. There were bees in the walls, and he cupped his hand against the beams and said, *Listen.*

I was tired and my feet, which always swell on airplanes, were too large for my shoes. The crumpled airmail envelope in my hand, its blue the color of the sky that scraped the top of the buildings, noted Ivetta's apartment number. I pressed it. Almost immediately, a voice answered: low, made of amber even in the machine's raspy throat. Ivetta was not in Sper-

longa, she was in Rome. She did not know when we were coming and so she had waited this morning for us to arrive. We
were to come up to the apartment.

The apartment was on the third floor of the building; it
was the sort of apartment which takes up one floor, so that the
elevator opened directly into the foyer. Later, in New York, I
would become acquainted with this kind of apartment, with
walking sticks and umbrellas helter-skelter in a stand, mail on
the table, and toile wallpaper in the foyer, always an apartment
which belonged to the parents of friends, and seemed unob-
tainable to anyone of our generation, like Studebakers, or pia-
nos with ivory keys, but then I found this exotic—it was like
stepping unprepared onto a stage. This room, too, was paved
in green marble. In the middle of the floor was a white marble
column, with a niche for a vase. The vase held a bouquet of
flowers made out of beads on twisted wires. Ivetta, whom I
had met a year before, in New Haven at my brother's gradu-
ation from college, was much as I remembered her: the two
separate eyes, the shock of gray hair with a white forelock, the
black clothes; today, a cashmere pullover, the neck stretched
out so that it hung like a cowl, black pegged trousers, and
black slippers. She wore thick silver hoops in her ears, and she
was smoking a kind of unfiltered cigarette I have seen only in
Italy, called Stop. The moment we entered the apartment she
began speaking. Her English was quick, idiomatic, and Italian, the penultimate word of each sentence emphasized with a
dip, a thickening of vowels that ended in a cocked consonant,
as if each phrase were itself a word: the effect was of running
feet, sliding into third base in a sandlot. She kissed me on each
cheek, but she had not met my husband and when I intro-

duced him she smiled and put out her hand. On her index finger she wore a silver ring with a large green stone. Her fourth finger was bare. My husband then—and now, still—has very large hands: he is a painter but he has worked as a commercial fisherman and as a builder, and his hands are muscular and covered with tiny scars. Now, years later, he is missing half of the index finger on his left hand, but then his hands were intact.

His beard, which he kept cropped short, was black then and he had a trick of staying very still and looking at you like a mythical beast, a griffin or a cat who might speak if you stayed very still. He used this look on Ivetta and not surprisingly she was affected by it. She took a step back, glanced at me with a look I can now see was at once affectionate and worried, as well as, for an instant, predatory, then threw up her hands. She was not, as we could see, she explained, in Sperlonga. She was here in Rome, because she did not want to leave the apartment. Indeed she had not left the apartment for a week, except to visit her mother in her villa in Trastevere. Did we want something to drink? We did. It was eleven o'clock in the morning. She left the foyer and emerged moments later with tall glasses filled with limonata and ice. She made the sign of the cross. Her mother was dying in Trastevere. The mint in the limonata was from her garden. In Trastevere, she told us, through the whole house, which was four stories and looked at the river with twelve eyes, all shutters were closed because her mother could no longer stand the light. She went every day and sat with her mother for three hours in the dark. She could not go to Sperlonga because her mother was dying. She crossed herself again. We were still standing in our traveling clothes among our bags, holding the tall sweaty glasses of limonata.

She was very sorry that she was still in Rome when we had expected to have the apartment to ourselves. We shook our heads: it was generous of her to have us in the apartment at all. Standing in the foyer, I could see that the apartment was very large. Two open doors leading away from the marble pillar showed vistas of long halls, in which some doors were open and some shut. At Ivetta's direction, it was down one of these corridors where we put our bags, in a square room painted pale green. The bed had a white coverlet. Two reading lamps were placed on either end of the headboard, which was padded in pale green damask.

We had left New York in a flurry of packing and arguments and at the moment all I wanted in the world was to lie down on the white bed and hone my skull against the green damask. The thought of being married tired me: I wanted to be alone so that I could see what I could make of it. I could feel my bones under my skin. The moment we put our bags by the door Ivetta called from the other end of the apartment. We must have something to eat! There was nothing for it. At the end of the hall Ivetta had laid out plates in the kitchen: cheese, olives, ham. She was paring off slices of bread onto a wooden board. The bread had come from the bakery near her mother's house, the bakery where she had gone as a girl. The olives were from Sperlonga. Had we been to Sperlonga? No? She sighed, wiping her hands free of bread crumbs on her trousers. Now that we were here in Rome, perhaps we should go.

Since we had just arrived in Rome there was no answer to

this. I ventured that she had said that she could not go to Sperlonga because her mother was dying in Trastevere. Her mother,
she said, had been dying for a long time. She made a sweeping
gesture with her hand, and the cigarette ash fell in an arc on
the table. Her mother could die forever, that was the truth.
The truth was that she had not gone to Sperlonga because
she did not want to go alone. Since my brother had written
to her, her husband of twenty-five years had left her, she had
discovered that he was in love with another woman—here she
used an exclamation in Italian that was unfamiliar to me—
a woman young enough to be his daughter, and she was in
the apartment in Rome because her mother had told her not
to leave the apartment because possession was nine tenths
of the law and the apartment was in the name of her husband. She could not stand it here in Rome. If she was in Rome
it was expected that she would go and see her mother every
day, in the dark house.

The kitchen was full of hot white light. Ivetta had drawn
the curtains, but they were white, sheer curtains smocked in
a honeycomb pattern. Diamonds of light danced on the white
walls, and the floor, which was also white pickled wood. I was
uninterested in food. When I get off an airplane I usually
feel for many hours as if my body were continuing to hurtle
through space—a body that should be fed on nitrogen gas, or
gasoline. My husband was famished. He made a huge sandwich with the bread, the cheese, and the ham—so it was just
as well that I was not very hungry.

The olives tasted of rosemary and smelled of tar. Ivetta
was drinking white wine. She asked about my brother and
about my parents, whom she had met. She was very fond of

my brother, who has a gift for languages. If he is on a train in a new country he can start the journey knowing a few tourist phrases—ticket, hotel, coffee, restaurant—and at his destination he will be discussing geology. My brother was trained as a geologist. I on the other hand have only schoolgirl French, which by now has been reduced to a small stock of endearments and imprecations. My ear for languages, unlike my brother's, is almost nonexistent. At school I was given a deferment from the language requirement, because I was hopeless. This was a sorrow to me. It is clear to me that an educated person speaks and reads four or five languages well; I speak and write only English, and often I find that what I mean to say, even in English, evades me or ends up meaning something I didn't intend to say at all.

My husband ate his sandwich. He had finished his limonata and Ivetta now poured coffee into espresso cups. The cups were white porcelain with gold rims. A great-aunt of mine, who lived in Palm Beach, had an identical set of cups, and for a moment the coincidence startled me. Once a few years later, after our daughter was born, I was sitting on a sofa in an apartment on Pierrepont Street, in Brooklyn, a street that led down to a windy playground from which my friend and I had just returned with our little girls. I noticed that the coffee table on which we had put our mugs and the children's spouted cups was the same table that had been in my grandmother's apartment in Chelsea, a mahogany oblong with gilded moldings and small claw feet.

You have my grandmother's table, I said. No, I do not, said my friend. It was a table she had found in a shop on Atlantic Avenue. The top was dusty and I ran my finger across it.

Those were the days when the children were small and there was so little time for things to be clean before they were covered again with juice and spilled milk. I wiped my fingers on my skirt, a patchwork blue cotton wrap skirt whose tie was forever coming undone. It was a twin to a similar skirt that I had lost and then replaced with this one, which then later turned up in a used-clothing store in Cambridge, when I went searching for treasure with the daughter, then on my lap, all grown up, confirming what we already knew: the things we love find us as we find them. That morning in Rome, with the light coming through the windows, Ivetta wiped her hands on her trousers and announced, as we sat sipping our coffee— too strong for me, but not for my husband, who had grown up with a drop of coffee in his milk—that after all, it was hot, she did not want to stay in Rome. So what if her husband was in Sperlonga? She wanted to go to Sperlonga and that was what she would do. We should see Sperlonga, she said, lighting her cigarette.

We would go that afternoon.

My husband and I looked at each other. We had planned to spend a week in Rome. We had no plans to go to Sperlonga. I had been to Rome once before without him, with a college boyfriend. What I remembered most clearly were heated exchanges about the price of pensiones, and walking around in the blazing sun in the Forum with a battered Blue Guide, pretending to be not a character in Henry James, but a character, I think now, in a Merchant Ivory production of a Henry James novel. I had read myself through *The Portrait of a Lady* in school, and pretended to love *What Maisie Knew,* but as Maisie, it was clear, knew more than I did at twenty, I had

given up. The first paragraph of *The Golden Bowl* I knew too
well; I had not recovered from making it known, in a class at
school, that I had confused that book with *The Golden Notebook,* which I had read and also misunderstood. We arranged
with Ivetta that we would go for three days with her, to Sperlonga, in her car. It would be easy to return to Rome by train,
she said. And who knew? She might be happy in Sperlonga
and stay for the month as she usually did. It would be impossible, she said, to be more unhappy in Sperlonga than she was
now in Rome, slinking around the apartment in her bathrobe,
summoned daily to Trastevere to sit with her mother, who
demanded items to be brought to her which were unattainable
in Rome at that time of year: figs, and chestnuts, as if it were
autumn, not the beginning of summer!

We went down the long cool hall to fetch our bags. Or
rather, my husband went to fetch them. I sat at the
table, eating a piece of lemon rind. Ivetta bustled around me,
folding tea cloths and swathing cheese and salami with plastic
wrap. She would take the food that was left with her, who
knew if she was coming back! And if her husband came back
to the apartment from wherever he was, why should she leave
perfectly good food for him to eat? Let him eat on his own,
she said. It occurred to me as I sat at the table that Ivetta
was going to Sperlonga to find her husband, perhaps to confront him in a public place. Once, in Perugia, on my first trip
to Italy, I had stayed with the boyfriend with whom I had
argued. When we returned we would argue for another year,
through the winter in Providence, where one week the family
in the house three doors down from us, in a house which was

a century older than ours and which they insisted on lighting with gas lamps, was bound and held at gunpoint. That summer in Perugia we sat every night in a piazza a stone's throw away from the Etruscan walls.

Each evening as dusk inked in first the lintels of the doorways and then the alleyways between the buildings, the fountain was circled by swallows, who rose like smoke signals over the jet of water that arced from the dragon's mouth: a dragon who put out his own fire. At six every evening, a boy drove his Vespa at top speed straight into the door of a house that faced the square. Night after night, idly, as we did everything then, we discussed the Vespa. Was there a courtyard past the door we could see where he parked it? A long hallway? Punctually, he whizzed past us into the doorway and disappeared. I wonder now why we waited to investigate the boy's wild aim at the doorway—it was a wooden doorway with a Della Robbia Madonna set over the putti and peeling arch—but when we did, one night when it was just beginning to rain in the piazza and so our dusk-lit twilight was cut short, we saw only a stone stairway three feet from the lintel, and then, nothing: a tattered straw mat, unraveling, had been placed just inside the door. When I thought now of Ivetta, standing in her kitchen in her black-and-white Marimekko apron, in Rome, thinking about going to confront her husband, I thought of those stone stairs, and the boy disappearing, as if into thin air, night after night after circling the fountain in Perugia.

My husband had collected our bags. While I waited with him Ivetta went to get her things. These were minimal. In a large straw basket embroidered with a pink straw flower, she had put the leftovers from the kitchen—the salami, the cheese, and half a loaf of bread wrapped in wax paper. She had changed from her house shoes, black espadrilles she wore as mules, with the back of the shoe tamped down under her heel, into a pair of red suede sneakers. In the other hand she carried a large-brimmed canvas hat. She assured us that we would love Sperlonga—there is no reason to stay in Rome! she said—and, anyway, you will be back!

My husband and I looked at each other. He was well acquainted with my unease, traveling. If anything, now I am more anxious. When I am not, or when I pretend not to be, I try to behave as if I were a person who could throw caution to the winds and stay anywhere, not knowing beforehand whether the room would be too small, or too ugly, or on a street I cannot imagine living on for one moment. The inability to travel easily is for me a symptom of anxiety. My character is essentially porous: the view outside the hotel room of the parking lot, past the windows that do not open and are very slightly grimy, could pass into my heart, accumulating grit and sorrow around the idea that not only I, but anyone, would have to stay here forever, with the plastic webbing of the carpet smelling of mold.

My husband and I had traveled before. We had spent three months in Italy, before we were married, in a house with a sleeping porch and narrow hallways in a village above Assisi, where Umbrian hills pressed into a cerulean sky, and I sat on a flat rock below the house and thought about all the wonderful things I would write if I really was a writer, rather than pretending to be one, when in truth I was a woman who wanted to have a baby. All day my notebook sat idle. It was May then, too, and cold, and I wore a very expensive fawn-colored shearling coat I had bought in Venice, with money I had earned at the magazine where I then worked, writing about clothes—one of the only things, then, that I knew a great deal about, along with passages from "The Waste Land" and some Yeats poems, which I liked to recite to myself, and a few lines from *Cymbeline,* which I had decided perversely was my favorite play, not knowing or understanding that it was not a young person's play and that I did not know the least thing about it: "I heard no letter from my master since I wrote him Imogene was slain."

As it got warmer, small lizards, some the color of spearmint and others a pale corn silk color that was almost clear as glass, darted over the rock and paused on my hand. I exchanged the shearling coat for a mohair sweater which itched, faintly, and kept me awake. We were not married, then, and I did not yet have a baby. We were trying on different houses and places to live, like wind-cheaters. Later, when I did have a baby, I would go back to Italy once more with her father, and with the baby, who was teething, and who tugged ferociously at the harness in her stroller because what she liked to do was to chase pigeons in the piazza, a baby with wide-set eyes who has grown up to hold a paintbrush between her teeth, as her father does, and like her mother, stare into space.

We went down in the elevator with Ivetta. Her car, it turned out—a brown Fiat sedan, with one door that would not open—was parked almost directly in front of the apartment house. The interior was hot, and the pages of *La Stampa* that covered the backseat were yellowed and smelled like burned cloth. I sat in the back, with the straw basket of food, to which Ivetta at the last minute had added some cold bottles of mineral water. My husband sat in the front, in the passenger seat. It occurred to me as I hunched in the back, my knees slightly drawn up under my "traveling" skirt—I still had ideas then about what was proper to travel in, and I was wearing a green skirt and a linen navy blouse with long sleeves, rolled up below my elbows, and flat shoes—that I had never before been in a car with my husband that he wasn't driving. At home we had a small red truck. It looked like a large model of a Matchbox car. Years later, when I married again, my stepson, who was maniacal as a child about cars, had hundreds of these: for years, my instep held the mark of those cars, from when I stepped on them at night, in the long dark hall of the apartment where we then lived. This truck was a stick shift. It was impossible for me to drive it. When I went up even a small slope in the seaside town where we then lived, down a long rackety road on the way to a studio that belonged to a famous painter, and about which, many years later, there would be a long protracted lawsuit which resulted in the view from that studio being ruined, I felt the weight of the truck behind me. Without fail, my reaction to the feel of this weight was to let go of the wheel and put my foot down on the accelerator. For a long time afterward I had not driven a car, and although I did not know it I was on the verge of a period of many years, more than two decades—in those days the idea of looking back on a decade through which I had lived had not occurred to me—in which I would not drive at all, until I was forced to by circumstance.

It was peculiar to be in the backseat. I could see the back of my husband's head. His black hair curled over the back of his corduroy jacket, which despite the heat he had not yet taken off, probably because his shirt was soaked with sweat, and I wanted to reach out and touch his shoulder. I did not. We did not touch each other very much in front of other people. In the front seat, Ivetta adjusted the rearview mirror, with displeasure. Her husband had driven this car last. He had the Peugeot now, wherever it was. She always asked him to readjust the mirror after he drove the car—the Fiat was her car—but did he? No. He did not.

There was no air-conditioning. We rolled the windows down. The town of Sperlonga is halfway between Rome and Naples, on the Tyrrhenian Sea. We drove south, along the Via Flacca. Umbrella pines lined the road. I had never seen them before but I knew exactly what they were; their limbs were as complicated as the spokes of parasols. As we drove past field after dry field, some gleaming with ginevra, which I found beautiful but I knew from my friend who lived above Assisi that farmers despised (the roots were matted and hard to pull up, the seeds traveled all over Italy and contaminated the fields), we began to see herds of buffalo, grazing, in fields marked off by umbrella pines. These fields were free of the gold clouds of ginevra. The grass was shorn and yellowing under the hot sky. The buffalo were milked for mozzarella di bufala. Strange, Ivetta, said, that we had not seen buffalo before: after all, we were Americans. The bottled water was now warm; we stopped at a *baretto* for more cold drinks. The bar also sold straw baskets and mats. There was a bag exactly like Ivetta's, with a pink flower, and I immediately wanted it: I wanted to be Italian, I wanted to have the sort of bag an Italian woman carried. The first time I had been in Rome, I had watched women walk slowly up the streets with their neatly

the sea. On the stucco wall of the courtyard directly facing the window was a blue-green eye, with a black pupil, that looked back into the blank windows of the house; the disembodied eye of Horus. The room we were to stay in—for how long? who knew?—was under the eaves. A ladder pulled down from the ceiling. There was a low wide bed under the beams that smelled of rusks. Fully clothed, I lay down on it. Early in the day when we had stopped for the cold drinks I had discovered that once again I was not going to have a baby. The knowledge both depressed me and lightened me. When I woke it was dark, my skirt was bunched under me, and my legs were bare.

We spent five days in Sperlonga. Every day we slept under the rafters until the sun and hunger woke us, and then we dressed in cool, light clothes and went to the bar in the piazza, where pink plastic chairs ringed tiny tables, and drank coffee. I pretended to read *La Repubblica,* from which I could make out, with effort, the headlines. My husband made charcoal and pencil drawings in a small book he carried in his pocket. He liked a particular kind of sketchbook with a hard, marbleized black cover, and as he drew he smoked the small cheroots his grandfather, who came from a town fifteen kilometers from here but which he refused to visit, had smoked. They were called *sports.* Sometimes he drew me, but I was an annoying model: I was restless, and my face set into an expression he found irritating. When we had first met he had drawn me endlessly; we lived then for a time on a pond filled with leeches and turtles, and we would take a green rowboat into the middle of that pond and he would draw and I would read. Sometimes I fell asleep. His great friend then was an older painter (he was younger then than my first husband is now), who had his daughters pose for him as nymphs, which they found not surprisingly to be boring in the extreme. To solve this problem he would nail books to the trees for them to read: the house on the pond where we lived belonged to him, and some of the books had gashes through their pages.

When we were finished with our morning coffee, we shopped for lunch in the market in the adjacent piazza. We bought tiny purple artichokes that Ivetta showed me how to cook, ninety percent of the leaves peeled off like pale green confetti, each denudation making a tiny bird click, and every day we bought fresh buffalo mozzarella from a tiny *latteria*. The animals were milked at dawn, and the cheese was made fresh every morning in a formidably clean kitchen behind the shop. On the second day I had asked to see it, and before I stepped into the kitchen the girl behind the counter took a clean cloth, rinsed it in soap and warm water, and gave it to me to wipe my hands. Later I would think of this when my first child was born, in the hospital nursery where I went to learn how to change her. I had never in my life before that moment changed a diaper. In my dressing gown covered with roses, which I had bought especially, I told the stern nurse—she was British, and had been present at the birth—that I'd washed my hands, and thought of the day in Sperlonga when I despaired of having a child: the mozzarella in the shop had smelled too of milk, and the baby had the same milky smell; and further back, to Eliza Doolittle, who said, "I washed me hands and face before I come." In that moment I had left behind whatever I had been before to be a mother, which I would be from then on. When the children were small they were terrified of *My Fair Lady:* it was the scene, we realized, of the bath.

The mozzarella, in its milky water, was sublime nursery food, tasting of grass and clouds. We ate it on the spot, with ends of bread we saved from breakfast. The third morning, after our coffee, we went for a swim. When we came for our cheese the girl behind the counter shrugged. The cheese was no good now. It was done. Finished. It was too hot in the middle of the day to swim or walk; at one in the afternoon all the shops closed, the pottery shop and the kiosk that sold postcards, the *latteria* and the *salumeria,* and we went back to the house and ate lunch with Ivetta. On one day, two of her cousins joined us, a man who owned a vineyard a little ways away, and who brought wine that tasted to me like leather, and his wife, who was also a cousin. They both had Ivetta's high brow and staccato way of speaking. To these cousins, in Italian, Ivetta lambasted her husband; the cousins agreed in vociferous voices, eating crespelle and tiny bits of sopressata, and shrimp marinated in hot pepper oil. Ivetta had one daughter and two sons, grown-up children; nevertheless, the cousins agreed, the marriage had been a mistake! She should have it annulled! Her cousin the vintner knew just the person. He would call him immediately! No, no, no—Ivetta waved her hands helplessly above her head. Perhaps he would see reason. Like Chiara's husband, the one who had the house that Tante Melina left?—her cousins nodded—maybe it's a phase? Ridiculous, running around like that!

I understood only a little of this. The leathery wine coated my throat. After lunch, we napped in the room under the eaves. When I could not sleep I picked at the stitching of the satin blanket cover, which I rolled up into a second pillow—it was too hot for a blanket. The room smelled of the straw which was used for insulation under the roof. I read, in a desultory way, *The Golden Bowl,* often just the opening lines, "The Prince had always liked his London, when it had come to him; he was one of the modern Romans who find by the Thames a more convincing image of the truth of the ancient state than any they have left by the Tiber." My copy, a paperback, had a detail from John Singer Sargent's *Repose* on the cover, a girl with a cloud of black hair, her head resting on a green sofa under a gold picture rail. Sometimes when I did sleep I would wake up and find my husband drawing me: I found this irritating—the pictures with my mouth open, and my hair in knots. Sometimes it was his gaze that woke me. In the afternoon, we went down the road to the beach.

Sperlonga is built on a promontory that faces the sea. Sometimes when we walked down the gravel drive to the beach from Ivetta's house—she never came with us, but worked on her translation of Pavese, in the afternoons—thin stripes of distant thunderstorms, deep purple, banded the horizon. The beach was unlike the beaches I knew, with high dunes and deserted strips of sand, where in May we walked fully dressed, in long pants and anoraks, backing up against the wind. Here it was hot and still. There were occasional small dogs on short leashes. The beach was narrow and backed up instead to kiosks that sold the inevitable aranciata, tiny glasses of wine, and stale paninis. To the west of our beach was the Grotto of Tiberius, built by the Emperor Tiberius, who loved the story of Odysseus and commissioned huge statues to commemorate his voyage, including his ship heaved into the waves by Scylla and the blinding of the Cyclops. On the beach I read on a raffia blanket and my husband drew: the sea, the distant grottos, the sentinel stone towers that ring the harbor. We brought *acqua minerale* and bought the aranciata, whose bitter pulp stuck in my teeth. Sometimes we bought small hard biscuits that reminded my husband of the biscuits his Aunt Jenny baked in Rhode Island when he was a child, which he sucked on like stones.

We stayed five days. We did not meet Ivetta's husband; by the third day, she said, he had returned to Rome. From the Sperlonga house, she told us, he had taken a beautiful mohair blanket that her aunt had given them as a present: "What do I need with a blanket?" she said, spitting. It did not occur to me or to my husband at the time that to listen to Ivetta's tale was odd, perhaps even dangerous, given that we were so recently married, nor did it seem to occur to her. In the evenings we sat with her in the little piazza where there were only small children kicking a ball but no boy with a Vespa mysteriously exiting at full speed, and people she had known all her life would come and speak to her, and commiserate, until the hour in the evening when she would seem to forget all about her calamity, and smoke her Stops.

Then it was time to leave. We wanted, after all, to be back in Rome, and from there to go to see our friend above Assisi, and to see if the waitress in Borgo San Sepolcro, who looked as if she herself stepped out of a Piero, was still there, with her blond hair pulled back and plaited into a sheaf of corn, in her gray turtleneck. On our last morning we had coffee with Ivetta in the piazza, and ate our milky cheese, *bocconcini* like small opals in a cup lined with leaves, and as I went to buy postcards I knew I wouldn't send, I realized I wanted a souvenir. Since it was still the beginning of the season many of the cubbyhole emporia that catered to tourists were closed, but there was one shop I had seen, down one of the bleached crab legs that led off from the high white shell of the Piazza della Repubblica. To its door, a little bell was attached. We rang it: Ivetta knew the owner; we went in. It was a treasure shop. There was some Murano glass, a tray of rings, a few pieces of dark heavy furniture, and a pair of earrings displayed on a piece of black velvet. The earrings were gold and shaped like shields, and in the center of each shield was a hummingbird's egg of coral. The shape of the earrings was perhaps fateful; Sperlonga, I knew, was famous for defending its treasures. In 1957, after Roman relics were found in the Grotto of Tiberius, the Sperlongani blocked the road to Rome to prevent them from being taken away. The earrings were eighteenth century, said the proprietor, who was quick to tell us that the shop was open because he was a true Sperlongani; he lived above the shop year-round, in the *centro storico.*

When I tried the earrings on, it was immediately clear to us all that in another life I had lost them and they were now being returned to me. I had come to Sperlonga, in this con-voluted way, with the man I had just married, hoping I was carrying a baby, with a woman whose husband had disap-peared as neatly as the boy on the Vespa had vanished night after night in another piazza into a house whose doorway was topped with an arch holding a Madonna. My husband turned my face to the light. In that moment I wanted the earrings more than I had wanted anything before. But it was early in our trip. What if our money ran out? What if I found some-thing else? The price came down; then it came down a little more. Anyway, it was never *un occhio della testa,* as the Italians say, an eye out of the head. Still, the next morning when we drove north in our rented car I was without them.

In Sperlonga they paint the evil eye on doors and ceilings to ward off misfortune. Perhaps that day in the almost empty town I was afraid of attracting its gaze by taking such an easy pleasure. But really, I think it was a zest for miserliness, for hedging bets, that accounted for my not buying the earrings, and for that I am ashamed. In his preface to *The Golden Bowl* James writes, "The whole conduct of life consists of things done, which do other things in turn." When we next heard from Ivetta, she wrote that the earrings were still in the shop; her mother was better; she had decided to stay, for a while, in Sperlonga; her husband had rented a different apartment in Rome, near San Giovanni—how he had the money she didn't know. When she next wrote, she mentioned neither the earrings nor her husband.

Some say the name Sperlonga means long hope. Later, I would have a brown-eyed daughter, and then quarrel irretrievably with her father, with whom I had sat in the green boat and who had smoked cheroots in the Piazza della Repubblica in Sperlonga, and much later, a blue-eyed one. They are both capable of tenderness and judgment. When I straighten out my jewelry, which I keep helter-skelter in an old shoe box, the girls say, Can I have this when you die? and laugh: I am their mother, I will never die. No one, yet, whom they love, has died. Often, dressing to go out, I have found myself searching for those earrings, as if I had bought them, so many years ago, and misplaced them.

Curious Yellow

Twice this week I've seen women wearing yellow stockings, each time at the wide intersection in my neighborhood across from the Columbia University gates, a crossing that like a piazza in an Umbrian painting is a headland, dropping as it does precipitously to the river. One woman was buying papers from the Indian news dealer, the other was going down the steps to the subway, and in each instance I thought of the first time I saw a pair of yellow stockings.

It was in the seventies, in Ken Russell's film *Women in Love.* Gudrun, played by Glenda Jackson, and her sister, Ursula (Jennie Linden), are walking away from the camera, down a lane bordered by green fields. Ursula's clothes are careless, ordinary, except for her marigold stockings. They are talking animatedly. Gudrun's love affair with Gerald, who later freezes to death in the snow, is doomed. The second feature that day was *Sunday Bloody Sunday* written by Penelope Gilliatt and directed by John Schlesinger. Again Glenda Jackson appeared, now as a woman in love with a boy who is loved with implacable yearning by an older man.

The films became one in my mind, and for some time after this when I thought of what the future held I saw Glenda Jackson in *Sunday Bloody Sunday,* magically wearing Ursula's yellow stockings, saying *damn,* and making coffee by running the hot water tap over the grounds.

In the middle of the years when I carried around this ridiculous image I acquired a shabby office in a big building down the hall from the woman who had written *Sunday Bloody Sunday,* and became a rapt audience for her stiletto humor and her elliptical charm. Once in a while during the winter an ancient, beautifully made mustard wool suit would make an appearance. Sometimes she wore it with yellow stockings, and this costume—far better than the pair of stockings I'd long ago bought and sometimes even wore—kept alive for me the green lane and the two women walking and talking, and the flash of color.

In the way of premonitions, this image turned out not to be so ridiculous. I was often rushing, running late, and if not running hot water over the grounds, even worse, gulping yesterday's cold coffee as I clattered out the door. In the middle of those same years, I also kept in my mind, like a watch fob—my grandfather had owned a watch like that, and my mother kept it on a stand in a small glass case—the opening sentence of a book by Doris Lessing, *The Golden Notebook,* "The two women were alone in the London flat," and, from a few pages later in that book, a paragraph about strawberries, which I wished I had written. Anna Wulf buys strawberries from a man selling them in the street; the man, like a truculent antihero in a novel by E. M. Forster, is angry at Anna that she is buying his strawberries: that is, that it is he who is selling them, and she who is buying them.

"With strawberries, wine, obviously," said Anna greedily; and moved the spoon about among the fruit, feeling its soft sliding resistance, and the slipperiness of the cream under a gritty crust of sugar. Molly swiftly filled glasses with wine and set them on the white sill. The sunlight crystallized beside each glass on the white paint in quivering lozenges of crimson and yellow light, and the two women sat in the sunlight, sighing with pleasure and stretching their legs in the thin warmth, looking at the colours of the fruit in the bright bowls and at the red wine.

For a long time, until I retrieved this passage, I thought that the berries that Anna is so greedily eating were in blue bowls. But the blue bowls, it turns out, are a figment. Why blue bowls? Why not white, or brown earthenware? Even now, rereading, I am looking for the blue bowls—the blue bowls that are missing from the paragraph, as if, having read it so long ago, so many times, it was not a page in a book but a page of my own life, the way I conflate the yellow stockings worn by Jennie Linden in a movie, starring Glenda Jackson, about women in love, with a movie in which Glenda Jackson also starred, which is also about men in love, with the author of the first movie who wrote, sometimes, and then less frequently, and then not at all, in the office next door to mine on a floor in an office building where people sat in offices either writing or not writing.

The office was located near Bryant Park, which then did not look anything the way it looks now. Now it looks like Paris. There are iron benches and places to buy coffee and tasty sandwiches, and in the winter there is a skating rink. Then, it was littered with crumpled newspapers and sad pigeons which no one fed. Like many parks in the city then it was frequented mainly by drug addicts; the parks were fens where it wasn't usual for ordinary people to go except at great risk, because they wanted something badly that they couldn't get somewhere else. Now the parks are clean and bright: Let's meet in the park! we say to each other when the weather is fine. Now there are other dark places instead, and sometimes those dark places have been eradicated by other kinds of drugs whose job it is to make ordinary people lose their sense of menace and sorrow.

One feature of that office building was that it was possible to walk from one street to another by crossing the long lobby. If you entered on Forty-third Street you could exit on Forty-fourth Street without going outside. I was fascinated by this. I wasn't alone in my fascination: it was a kind of urban sleight of hand, in which the way out could always be other than the way in, in which nothing was a dead end; where there was always light at the end of the tunnel. Upstairs, on the eighteenth and nineteenth floors, where we had our warren of offices, this glint was a matter of fact: a mirror had been placed at the corner where the corridors intersected at right angles, to keep people from running into each other. Another reason for this was to enable the editor of the magazine to evade writers who might want to speak to him, but the result was that as you walked down the hall you encountered yourself, and often bumped into your own reflection. That this was a metaphor was not lost on anyone.

I alternately spent my days staring out the window and writing about garbage scows in the river and newfangled pocket knives and the Irish Troubles and frocks that cost more than cars, and one day an exasperated colleague, a few years older than I, a man who wrote about race riots and the fall of governments, said to me, "Write what happened, not what happened to you," and I had no idea what he was talking about, and I stopped, for months, writing anything at all: I stopped seeing from one end of the corridor to the other. Around me in offices identical to mine women who were a decade or two older were teetering in lives whose common denominators were quick wit, cigarettes, divorce, suicide, and the kind of burnishing despair that takes an edge off gloss. When I walked down the hall I saw my reflection coming at me in the mirror. What was true about what they wrote about their lives, and what was not? I was too young to ask, or to know, or to know how to ask, or even to form that question. What mattered was not what was said, but how: the what was incurable, anyhow. After a time I began to write, instead, about other people, and one of those people was an artist who was interested in light: in one piece, a lantern projected the image of a window filled with yellow light on the wall. It looked as if the image were cast by a real window when it was not, and since then, whenever I see the light cast by a window on a nearby wall, I think of his image of imaginary yellow light. He was from Iceland, where it is cold and dark, and where people can freeze to death, in the snow.

In time the magazine for which I worked no longer had its offices in that building, and before we left, I retrieved the clock that had ticked in the eighteenth-floor hall, and hung it in my kitchen. Soon afterward I left the magazine, and then returned, and then left again, which is another story. But when I first started there—it was my first real job—within weeks it seemed inconceivable that I could ever work anywhere else, nor

did I think I would, or could. This premise failed, as do most
love affairs which are based on fate and ardor: I was not aware
then that I was on the brink of a world that was about to end,
as the writer in the mustard suit told me, when it did, "Not
with a banger, but with a wimpy," deflecting as she knew how
to do, grief with wit.

In all the years that followed I did not return to that building, until recently. It was now filled with other tenants. I had a
meeting there, to discuss finances, at which I have never been
very adept. That lack of dexterity had resulted in the meeting, in which it was made clear to me that drastic measures
needed to be taken, measures that would mean breaking up
the house where I had lived where the clock ticked merrily
in the kitchen over the blue pantry door. But although I had
been given the address twice over the phone, I'd lost it. On the
way there I had had to call and be told the address for a third
time; even then, I transposed the numbers until I was under
the awning, where almost every day more than two decades
ago, the man I was in love with waited for me at lunchtime,
cupping his hands to keep the yellow feather of the match he
was lighting out of the wind that snaked off Sixth Avenue.
We would go, later that evening, to see *I Am Curious (Yellow),* or *Badlands,* or *Les enfants du paradis,* fifty blocks uptown,
on Ninety-fourth Street, at the Thalia. The filthy seats in the
theater tilted backward, so that the images on the screen
threatened to topple and smother you.

I was very young when I began to come every day to that
building. To return was to dive into a sea from which I had
never emerged; a body of water in which I had barely sprouted
limbs. The elevator was a bathysphere. It was a grand joke: to

arrive there for a meeting whose subject was fecklessness, in the very place where I had learned and tried to resist the pull of that particular cataract—a life in which an angular woman nearing middle age, invented by a woman who kept a mustard suit for thirty years, would try to divest herself of longing in a London flat by grinding her foot into cigarette ash that had fallen onto her carpet. The kind of woman who would herself keep a mustard suit for thirty years, because it was a very good suit and she didn't have the money to replace it. A woman wearing yellow stockings the color of candlelight whose lover would freeze death.

A view from one street into another. A ridiculous image that, because I carried it with me, became true. When I began to keep house myself, I bought blue bowls because I thought that the strawberries eaten so greedily by Anna Wulf had been eaten from blue bowls, encrusted with sugar.

When I reread the passage I also knew that the two women talking animatedly in *Women in Love,* for me, had also become the two women alone in the London flat, and that Anna Wulf, who is waiting for Richard, the father of her child, to whom she is no longer married, had become Glenda Jackson in *Sunday Bloody Sunday,* who, when she takes care of five children for friends on the weekend, narrowly escapes losing one of those children—the eldest child, the officious one—when the dog, for which she is also responsible, runs into the street and is killed. And it was lost on me, then, that the real image I would take away from that film wasn't the woman grinding out her cigarette in the carpet, but the mayhem of years spent with children, that would influence what I made of my life.

What does it mean to conflate? Is it to tell lies? Much later, when I read Antonia Byatt's novel *Babel Tower,* in a chapter toward the middle of the book it is brought home to the protagonist, Frederica, by her lawyer, that she is in danger of losing custody of her child if she continues to insist on living with a man with whom she is in love, whose name is Richard. In a previous novel, *Still Life,* Frederica's sister, Stephanie, who is more lovable than she, less wiry, less intensely preoccupied, not inclined, as is Frederica, to calling old friends from pay telephones in the middle of the night, is electrocuted when she looks under her refrigerator, which is not grounded, for a wedding ring which has slipped off her finger. When in our old apartment we finally bought a new refrigerator, after years of bailing out the vegetable bin with a measuring cup, we found among the lost things underneath, barrettes tiny enough to hold baby hair, a silver cake spoon, a bank card belonging to my daughter's father, pencils embossed with the names of schools the children hadn't attended in years, and the skeleton of a baby bat. Was it a bat? Or was it a mouse? Or was that a mouse found elsewhere? And all the while I thought, sweeping it up, deciding what to save, *Be careful.*

Frederica, like Glenda Jackson in *Sunday Bloody Sunday,* has red hair. Does she, in the novel, as I think she does, wear yellow stockings? Am I misremembering? Thinking about this, I go down to the kitchen to look for the blue bowls, which are not there. When I watched the movie with two of my daughters, who between them have two mothers and two fathers, in the bottom of the house where they grew up, they were bewildered: Why does she stay with him if he is so awful to her? they asked, and marveled at the telephone wires connecting London and the old-fashioned answering service. That two men loved each other was not interesting to them.

In the house where I live now, east of the windy intersection and the park, the blue bowls I bought years ago quiver in lozenges of yellow light, a fiction born of a fiction. What was it, after all, that happened? One day in the office building I heard a thud next door, and went to check. She was wearing a brown suit, not the yellow one. Her red hair was the color of autumn leaves. I was very young, and it was the first time I had seen someone unconscious. I picked up the telephone. Twenty-five years later, a doppelgänger of that yellow suit turned up in a mail-order catalogue, as the "Sulfur Notre Dame Suit," and I folded down the corner of the page. Outside the door in the house where I am now, two thousand miles away, in the San Juan Mountains, where I am because—because I am away from home, it is summer, and the children have scattered—hummingbirds dive at a feeder filled with sugar water. The yellow one is the avenger; his whir is the deepest. Greedy, he wants the sugar water the most. "If this were played upon a stage now, I could condemn it as an improbable fiction," says Fabian to Malvolio, who has been tricked into wearing yellow stockings. Yellow the color of old nicotine stains, yellow as a condiment, saffron, lemon, honey, turmeric, nothing substantial, not something to make a meal on, but no less for that a mark of Helios, the sharp and sustaining sun.

Curtains

For almost a decade I lived in an apartment the size of a shoe box on West End Avenue which had three windows which fronted on a brick wall. These windows were bare because I was unable to reproduce in my apartment the curtains that in a life spent gazing out windows had made the greatest impression on me. The first two sets had hung, respectively and almost identically, in the music room of my glamorous piano teacher on Long Island and in the Elysian apartment of my great-aunt on Eighty-eighth Street. These curtains were pale green Scalamandré silk, with tiebacks. They were cool, remote, elegant, while I was heated, untidy, adolescent; and both housed, when I was a girl, daughters whom I wished I could be. The first was a huge, three-story stucco house on a sloping tree-lined street, with a green-tiled roof and concrete steps that led up from the sidewalk to a small veranda that served as a porch. I knew those steps quite as well as I knew the big oak door with the doorbell, which, unusual for those days, even, was an actual bell on a pull chain, because my piano teacher's house was the first place I was allowed to walk to by myself. This was such a novelty that I felt more unsure, on the way there, than I was. Although there was no house on the street that resembled it in any particular, I memorized each crack in the steps and the flagstones, and my fingers remembered the slightly convex ivory bell push, which did not work: one had to remember to pull the bell rope. I was so enamored of being by myself that often I would lean my head against the door and smell the paint's odor of oily tobacco. I knew that my mother thought the house was a disgrace. In the summer, joe-pye weed grew up through the cracks. It was a testament to her forbearance that I was allowed to go. Once I'd idly plucked some. It was in my hand when my piano teacher came to open the door, and she told me it was also called Queen of the Meadow.

She was the first and last person I knew for many years who had my initials, and she often exclaimed over the coincidence. We were in a club, she implied, with our rhyming letters, which sounded when she said them like a spoon hitting a triangle: sharp and clear. Twins! she would exclaim, and I'd shake my head. I was twelve, dark, moody. She was then perhaps forty. She wore her red hair in a snood; her clothes, as far as I remember, consisted of Rosalind Russell suits in violet and gray bouclé wool. On the landing I could see from the living room, where I sat week after week at the piano, enrobed in the smell of wax and Shalimar (I knew it was Shalimar because my mother wore it too, but only in the evenings, when she went out), there was a huge white wicker chair with a heart-shaped back; in each half of the heart was a wicker peacock, seen from the side. For her, I played Clementi and Haydn and Bach, badly. On the piano was a photograph of my piano teacher's husband, in an army uniform: I knew almost no one who had been in the army. In all the years I came to the house I saw him only once, handsome, sinewy, with the air some family men used to have of competence: he was lying on the ground under a car in the driveway. They had five children, which was unusual in the neighborhood. Later, I was friends with one of her sons who was a few years ahead of me in school: playing on a zip line in a neighbor's yard, he fell and broke his jaw.

But by his sister Vivian, I was transfixed. Once in a while, she would come and stay when my parents went out—even then I knew that for my mother, Vivian was a last resort. She was fifteen, wore her lank hair over one eye and an old green suede jacket, and she smelled of cigarettes. I was to call her Vi. The last time she came, she told me that I was old enough to watch over my brother and sister upstairs if I didn't fall asleep. She crept out of the house promising to return, and I watched her go, through the living room's heavy curtains, a hunched figure in the dark street. She came back an hour later. Her hair was wilder and another smell clung to her, one that would take me years to identify, muskier, unaired. We went into the kitchen, where all the lights were on, and she rattled between the stove and the table, talking fast. She was in love. It didn't matter who he was; he lived a mile away, she had walked—it was rainy, did I know it was raining—she found some pebbles from the driveway to throw up at his window, yes, she knew which one it was—she would have died if he hadn't come down. As she ricocheted between the stove and the table she picked up one thing and then another; by the end of her account she was holding a fork, which she drove into her hand, just hard enough to break the skin. I knew even then, as she held her hand under the kitchen tap, that Vivian had hurt herself because she was afraid of being hurt by this boy, whoever he was; I knew that he could not be anyone I could or would know, even though he lived one mile away. I was twelve. I was wearing a nightgown printed with little baskets filled with apples. I felt exhausted by what lay ahead. I went to sleep shortly afterward, to the quick sound of Vivian's voice on the telephone and then the scraping noise of my parents' key in the lock, and the sound of the curtains being drawn along the long rod in the living room, closing up the place where I had stood.

The pale green curtains at Vivian's mother's house—how odd, that she should be at once Vivian's mother and my piano teacher—looked out onto a patio furnished with elaborate white painted iron furniture. (Now that I have an untidy garden of my own, I know how difficult it is to keep up such furniture, with its curved menacing arms and mincing feet.) Identical curtains hung in my great-aunt's apartment on East Eighty-eighth Street, a few houses off Fifth Avenue, by the huge white snail of the Guggenheim Museum. These curtains flanked two long windows that looked across through the plane trees to a facing building across the street. They were the color of the underside of a leaf, muted, almost shiny, the silk webbed with tiny spun fibers. By the time I was old enough to remember other people's lives, the apartment was inhabited by my great-aunt and -uncle; my aunt, who was dark, quick, and elegant as a dragonfly, was the youngest sister of my paternal grandfather: there were almost twenty years between them. In one photo that hung in the apartment she is dressed in a pinafore with big round buttons. She is three, and has a pony on a lead. My great-uncle was the only other army man I knew. In the war, he'd been a marine. The family was given to large lapses of time between progeny. My aunt and uncle had two children, a son, who drew beautifully and disappeared to live in Alaska, who was ancient before I can remember him, and his sister, whom I adored. I knew immediately even as a small child that my uncle loved women: his wife, his daughter, and me, with wry reverence. He loved clothes and shoes, and scent. My aunt's clothes, like my piano teacher's, were beautiful. They were in very much the same style: fitted suits, Dior waists, hats from Hattie Carnegie.

Many years later when she was old she called me and asked me to come to see her. I was then living in the apartment which I had bought in part because the black-and-white Vermeer floor in the lobby reminded me of the black-and-white tiled floor of her dining room. When I arrived she brought me into the bedroom. The wall in the dressing room was lined knee high in white shelves with sliding doors, which had been especially made, I knew, to hold her shoes. "Here," she said, "take them." Evening pumps with diamanté buttons, by Delman, sandals with high heels by Roger Vivier. Almost none of them fit, but I scooped them up and took them home, where my daughters claimed a few pairs and the rest went into the dress-up box. In my aunt's mind, I knew, shoes were a close cousin to destiny: when she was fourteen and went out to work, one day—it was Indian summer, because heat figures in the story—the heel broke off her shoe, and she had enough—a nickel—to either fix the shoe or take the long trolley ride home, but not both: out of her wages her mother had given her trolley fare but kept the rest. She fixed the shoe. But by the time she walked home the other heel had broken, and she limped down Broadway. When she got home she told her mother she had to keep back ten cents a day for herself. Even at eighty, telling the story, she flushed: the peculiar family mix of guilt and desperation to keep something, anything, for oneself. Into my thirties, she always asked me if I had enough for a taxi; when once I looked in despair at myself in her hall mirror, at a coat I was wearing that was covered in cat hair and the remnants of a child's ice cream, which had melted onto my shoulder on the Eighty-sixth Street bus, she immediately gave me, from her closet, a velvet double-breasted Chesterfield the color of blue flax. Some people's lives occur on moving conveyances, and my aunt was one of these people.

Ten years after she lost the heel on her shoe, she fell in love with my uncle during a summer job waitressing in the country. After an argument they parted, enraged. A family of raised voices and not speaking. Some months later on a crowded trolley, she saw a familiar set of knees in front of her. He lowered his newspaper and asked her to marry him. A story at the dining room table, another argument: Is that the way it happened? It's the way I remember it. The heat of the day she lost her heel, and the heat of the argument, like a prickly rash, hot to the touch. My grandmother liked to tell it, and then, how my aunt, my father's sister, danced on the dining room table when my great-uncle came back from the war. He gave her a nickel. Outrageous! When I was very small my aunts and my grandmother would still argue about whether it was permissible to throw coins down to the street, eighty years ago, through the parted curtains of my great-grandmother's tenement apartment, to the street musicians who sang for their supper below.

I have never seen the trouble with clothes worn by others, perhaps because so early for me the clothes that I inherited from my cousin, I loved. She was four years older and infinitely sleeker than I was, and she had her own skate key, which she sometimes let me borrow when we were taken on a long car ride to Bear Mountain outside the city, where my aunt, who loved skating, would stand on the side of the rink in her fur hat and clap her hands when it grew dark and it was time for us to rush in, the snow gravelly underneath our runners, which had a harsh tang when we wiped our fingers along the pronged blades. I remember a party dress with a Battenberg lace bodice, and a tulle skirt the color of old honey. When I was twelve and she was sixteen she suddenly grew beyond me. In art class in school we had bathed photographs in the darkroom and watched images emerge, like creatures crawling out on land: pictures of ourselves mainly, or the trees in the schoolyard, predactyl, ganglia in the gray proto-light. With my cousin it was the reverse. She grew sleeker and stranger. In one photograph I still have of her she is in a white nightgown, posed in a doorway. Asleep or awake? Soon I would vanish into my own world, and those curtains would come down too, but I didn't know that yet. I wanted to be her, to have grown up in the house behind the green curtains, with my own skate key, and to choose where to step on the piano-key floor tiles, black, white, black, white, where when we were girls we shot hazelnuts, and counted the numbers of squares they crossed, and won pennies for our trouble.

The third set of curtains on which I set my heart I had seen only in a photograph. They belonged to Isak Dinesen, the Baroness Blixen. They hung in her house outside Copenhagen, a trio of doubled lace curtains that hung from high rods and pooled on the floor. Decades after seeing this photograph, a few hours before a flight out of Copenhagen to New York,

I paid a taxi driver to take me to Dinesen's house, which, as he pointed out on his GPS, was directly out of the way of the airport. Isn't there somewhere else, he asked, that you would like to go? There was not. It was raining. The rain clung to the windshield, to the trees. On our right for a while were high-peaked Danish houses, fronting the sea. The roofs looked like wimples. It was green, green, green: I had never seen so much green so close to salt water. The opposite, I imagined, of Africa. When we arrived at the house—the drive took about forty-five minutes—the gravel drive was wet. The tiger's-eye pebbles glittered. Although the driver had grown up in Copenhagen, he had never been to Dinesen's house. He knew all about her, though. He had read *Seven Gothic Tales* at school, and he had seen the movie. Over some details of this, he shook his head. We went in together, wiping our shoes carefully on the rubber mat the Dinesen Foundation had provided. Room after room of flat rugs, blue and white—I have similar rugs in the hallways of my house, even now—the smell of lemon and furniture wax, flowers from Dinesen's garden whose great-grandparents she had planted: lupine and oxeye daisies. The lace curtains puddled on the floor, exactly as they did in the photograph. I was in Copenhagen to interview the artist who worked with light. In his first project, he poked holes in a garden hose so that the water sprayed, shone a light on it, and called the rainbow *Beauty.* It started to rain again. The world outside the long windows was watered green silk. By now, I knew that the taxi driver's name was Lars. Looking out the window he took some of the lace in his hand, and said a word in Danish whose equivalent in English we determined on the way to the airport: "petticoat."

When I moved from the apartment the size of the boot box I moved to one with eleven windows. At that time, I was married to a painter and green was seldom allowed in my household. It was a color he found both irritating and enrapturing, and he would have none of it. In New York, lace would turn to rags of soot within days. Nevertheless, when I moved into that apartment with eleven windows, as if in a dream, curtains—neither silk nor lace—appeared on almost all of them. They came in pairs, like couples arriving for a dinner party for which I couldn't recall issuing invitations.

The bedroom was the first enshrouded. Shortly after my husband and I moved in, a friend, an owner of coasters and blanket covers, now almost ten years dead, and in whose house I am writing this, by a series of accidents, announced that her old dining room curtains would fit the bedroom windows. They arrived the next day, heavy, lined, the color of milky tea. Sometime after this, I had a baby, and the curtains in her room, too, came about by serendipity. As new mothers do, I moved through the days like a somnambulist. One afternoon—it was after I had left a job that I loved, and the world seemed to be perpetually starting and ending, like the sirocco—I found myself in a shop on Madison Avenue, buying, for the price of a ticket to Paris, seven yards of printed cotton, which my mother immediately identified as an almost exact replica of the curtains that had hung in my room as a child. I hadn't remembered, or had I? The kitchen then had a shade, the bathroom window was frosted glass: only the windows that faced east, across Harlem, were bare. One day, rummaging in the hall closet, I found white voile curtains that the previous owners had left. Two pairs fit the dining room; the last pair was too short for the study. Wantonly, I pulled down the hems; the little holes left a pretty row of eyelet. In a well-run house, by autumn, those curtains would have been changed to velvet, snug against the cold. But once up, the voile, a measure born of impulse, stayed. Everything stirred them.

September

The Thursday before, I received a telephone call from the children's school. There was a new family coming to the school. The elder child, a boy, would be in my children's grade. That year they were eight, or nine. They were in fourth grade. The school that they went to then was on the grounds of the Cathedral of Saint John the Divine, which was a few blocks from where we lived, in Morningside Heights, north of Central Park. To get to school we walked a few blocks south, past the Church of Notre Dame, which was built on a piece of rose quartz, and skirted through the back lot of the cathedral. At that time the back lot was a mess. Weeds grew helter-skelter through the broken tarmac. The blacktop itself was littered with stone carvings of angels and griffins; a stone-carver's workshop opened onto the back lot. It was managed by a man called Simon, who wore his hair in gray corkscrew curls. He was continually covered with marble dust. He had a fine face that verged on beauty, and looked like an angel who had fallen to earth.

Every morning we walked through the stone yard and then through the north transept door of the cathedral, and crossed the apse. Our neighbor also brought her child to school. She had a little dog, and the dog crossed the cathedral with us. Later, the north transept door was locked, and dogs were no longer allowed to walk through the cathedral at 8 a.m., but then we had the freedom of the place. There were peacocks on the close and at that hour they were often screaming. The year before, the graduating class had added an albino peacock to the flock. He had ceased to be a marvel, but it was still possible to be caught unawares at the sight of him. That was the first year that the children sang in the cathedral choir: you had to be nine, so I guess they were nine. Three afternoons a week they practiced in a room with casement windows in the south wing of the cathedral, which had once been an orphan asylum. On Sundays they sang at the eleven o'clock mass. Sometimes they also sang at evensong. They wore crimson robes and white collars, which were starched. Later, they would hate everything about choir: the rehearsals, the too-hot robe, and they wrote us long letters arguing their position which they read aloud to us at the kitchen table. By then we had moved to a house below the park which we could see from our window, and the cathedral and the life of the school had become more remote to them, and we drove them to school instead of walking through the apse. But that was later.

Then, it was the tail end of summer. It was very hot in the city. The leaves on the trees were dry, and when even a slight breeze moved them they rattled, as if a snake were moving through the branches. The sprinklers were turned on in the pocket park across the street. Water sizzled when it hit the blacktop. It was too hot to go without shoes, and when I took the children to play in the city sprinkler I kept my rubber flip-flops on. The ice cream truck jangled on the corner. It was the summer that we discovered that the owner of the truck was selling crack out of the back. As we did every summer, we had spent August at the beach. As usual, when we returned to our building, with its cool black-and-white-tiled lobby and our apartment with its long hall, and its view of the sprinkler and the ice cream truck, it was for the children as if we had never been away, or as if we had been away for a day and come back. On that Thursday we had been back four days. The telephone rang when we were walking in the door, and as I picked up the phone I was admonishing the children. I did not want water in the hall. I had left a fan on in the kitchen and the mail, which had been left on the counter, had blown down onto the floor, and the children were stepping on it with their wet feet. The voice on the other end of the telephone was known to me: it was the receptionist at the school, who was already at her desk although school had not officially opened. She wrote poems; it was that kind of school. She also acted, informally, as the school nurse—it was a small school. One of the children, who was prone to stomachaches, often took up the small cot behind her desk, especially when toward winter it got dark early. She told me about the new family, between pauses while I tried to get the children to pick up the mail, and to get the wet jellies off the baby, who was two. She gave me a telephone number, and said, "Promise you'll call." I promised. The idea was that before school opened these children would have met my children, and the mother, whom the receptionist said seemed shy, and whose husband worked long hours, would have met me.

It was Thursday afternoon. On Friday my mother called and suggested that the older children visit her on Long Island. It was hot, she pointed out, and they could swim in the pool. We drove them out that evening through the weekend traffic and then drove back into the city with the baby strapped into her car seat, and had drinks in the kitchen with a lot of ice. Then we put all the fans in the apartment in one room and the three of us slept fitfully. The next day we decided to go to the beach, to Sandy Hook, where we had never been, and we piled the baby back in the car with juice and towels and sandwiches. I missed the beach. Whenever we returned I pined for weeks. During those weeks I had fitful, disjointed conversations with my friend Anne, who rented a house near our rented house every August. We discussed, aimlessly, why we lived in the city, and what a bad idea that was until the weather got colder and we were distracted. That Saturday, the drive south into New Jersey took two hours, and the parking lots were full, except for one at the end. The baby ran into the waves and we pulled her back. I didn't think of the phone call I was meant to make, or even the other children, who were with my mother and, I assumed, adequately taken care of. The water was as warm as glass, and after a while we piled back into the car and drove back into the city, which by now was so overheated that from the highway it looked as though it were wreathed in smoke. When we got home we ordered Chinese food and the baby ate fried rice, which is what she orders to this day, and in the morning my husband drove out to fetch the children before the traffic got really bad. The next morning it was Monday, and I thought: I will meet her at school, and we will exchange numbers, because I hadn't called. The children wore uniforms at their school and, of course, the ones they had worn before the summer did not fit, but *would have to do,* which both they and I saw as further proof, as if any were needed, of my general mismanagement and inability to acquit myself as a bona fide mother, a mother who could make timely phone calls, who never broke promises, who would have ordered new uniforms in June, in the correct sizes, and in plenty of time, before we went away, to exchange them if necessary.

The next morning was school. We set the alarm and the children struggled into their too-small uniforms, and we set out down the street in the sun, which was already hot. Because it was the first day of school, the sitter, who took care of the baby, came early, so that I could walk the children to school and pay full attention to their new classrooms, where their names were written in construction paper, cut to look like bubbles, on the glass door. The new boy was in Jack's class. His uniform fit. He was shy, but friendly. On the way to school I had managed to remember his name, and to ask Jack to be especially nice to him. Think what it would be like to come to a new school, I said, and not know anyone! When the children were settled in their classrooms I walked out of the door of the school and down the long drive that ended at Amsterdam Avenue. It was 9:05 in the morning. The path had been embellished with late lilies, orange and cream colored, with black throats. At that time I had an office in the triforium of the cathedral in which I could sit by myself and write. It had been given to me by the Dean, whom I loved. I walked on the sidewalk on Amsterdam and crossed over to the wide flat steps of the cathedral, which as usual was flanked by tour buses. There was a group of Chinese tourists fanning themselves on the steps, and as I walked past them my way was blocked by a woman whom I knew was crazy. She was dressed in a white djellaba and a gold turban and she wore no shoes. She often spoke in tongues, and I assumed that she was speaking in tongues now, although it did occur to me in those seconds that she had never touched me before, as she did now, holding on to my arm with clenched fingers. Later I would notice I had a bruise but it was much later, weeks later, that I remembered her hand on my arm, and her knuckles, iron under the stretched skin.

She let go of my arm when I walked into the cathedral's cavernous cool, its smell of mold and incense, and something else my children called bat-wing, and there was Christopher, who worked in the cathedral, moving the chairs. The cathedral is huge, there are a lot of chairs, and it is his job to move them. He looked at me, and said, *Oh, miss,* and I said, *What's happened?* And then I knew.

In the days and weeks that followed in New York the heat did not let up. Sometimes it rained. Because no one could bear to be apart we had picnics with the children in the park, to which some people did not come because they thought the ash would cover us, and then as it got colder we sat in each other's apartments and cooked elaborate meals, and fed the children pasta, and decided whether we would stay in the city or whether we would leave. For weeks there were memorial services at the cathedral or downtown almost every day, and along with their book bags and baseball mitts and science projects, the children carried their crimson robes and starched white collars to school, where they were excused from classes to sing. Though I tried to invite the little boy who was new to the school to come and play, he would not come because he would not leave his mother. We did not meet his father, who that morning had disappeared like others into—nothing. Earlier that week, before school started, he had taken her wedding ring to a jeweler because he wanted it inscribed for their anniversary: he had the ticket in his pocket and though there was a story in the newspaper about it, it was never discovered where he had taken the ring and so it was lost. Because she refused to believe he was dead the funeral was not held for some weeks, and she insisted on an open empty coffin. I went to the funeral with a friend whose husband himself was dying, of cancer, and on the way home she told me that she wasn't going to let him die, what she said was "I am going to lay down in the middle of the road." He did die a year later and she died, too, shortly afterward, one falling after the other, but we didn't know that then, as we didn't know so many things—what had happened or what would happen. When later that winter, after the cathedral had almost burned to the ground, which is another story, my hands were cold after peeling some shrimp in the kitchen and my wedding ring flew off, and the children hunted for it all over the floor until Jack found it by standing in his stocking feet on a chair, on top of the icebox, I thought of her missing ring, and another story, of a woman in a novel who searching for her wedding ring under an icebox was electrocuted.

That weekend in September when we went to Sandy Hook, because I was dissatisfied with my life, and angry at having to live it, and to have summer end, we drove down through the long cattails and I was unhappy because the beach that I love doesn't have cattails. I didn't like the boardwalk, or that the water was warm. The baby didn't care. She was thrilled to be at the beach and to see the tiny crabs burrowing in the sand. She drank her red juice right from the bottle, and it made a red mark around her mouth, and I remember being tired of juice and juice boxes, and the heat. The baby tracked sand over the towels with her wet feet, and I looked across the water to where we could see New York City, gray with dust rising up in its stone cauldron, and I said, "The last thing I want to see when I go to the beach is the Twin Towers." That is what I said.

An Enlarged Heart

It began with a cough. Her brother had a cough. And, after all, what was a cough? They had all had them. In the winter, they passed them around like sweets. Enough coughing meant no school. Although sometimes we sent them off anyway—risking a call from the school nurse, who only half the time would be convinced by our pleading that it was nothing—so that a few more hours might elapse before the apartment filled with their books and the paper wrappers from their snacks.

But now it was August, and we were at the beach. All winter we dreamed of the house, with its blue floors, the tiny periscope hole in the roof, the red chairs, the rickety porch with its view of the bay. The children turned brown. The sea was flat. At low tide, a little pool appeared, and a sandbar, and she, the youngest at three, stood on tiptoe in the water, screeching when an inch-high wave hit. "I think the water's actually cold," she ran to tell us. "No, I think it's actually warm." We sat by the edge in our low beach chairs, the same chairs that used to embarrass us when our parents brought them to the beach. Why do we have so much stuff? we would ask them, eager to be free of it all, the towels and swimsuits and bottles of juice and fruit, imagining ourselves alone on an empty stretch of beach, naked, with a rucksack. Now we're the ones who unload the car and carry the heaviest bags.

She's so little we let her run naked, even though we have learned that turning brown is bad. We are careless, self-indulgent, to let her do it. By late afternoon, the sun has slipped behind the enormous high dunes, and blue shadows lap at the water. When she comes up from the edge, she is shivering. Her older sisters and brother and their friends are far out in the waves, on their boogie boards and surfboards, unidentifiable in their black wetsuits. We keep track by counting. Is that Anna? We ask each other: Do you see Nick? There's Rose. "Come in now! Come in!" we scream at them, our arms making huge pinwheels so they will pay attention. It is easy for them to pretend they don't see us.

During the night, she coughs on and off, and wakes once. The wind on the bluff pounds the house. In the morning, it is hot and blue again. We get to the beach after lunch, but the sun is still high. From the top of the dune, shielding our eyes, we look for the cluster of bright umbrellas that mark the colony of our friends. They hail us. The older children jump like seals into the waves and swim out to their pals. She stays by the edge. Today, there is another child her age, but she's cranky and won't play. It's too much sun, she didn't sleep, we explain to the other child's parents. Secretly, we are annoyed: Why won't she just play nicely? The younger children are fooling around with the surfboard, and she wants to try. A wave rears up suddenly, a dragon, foaming at the mouth, and she's hurled underwater and onto the sand. Everyone races to help. How can we have allowed this to happen? This is appalling!

She is young, much too young for these high jinks. She comes up sputtering. What kind of parents are we? Until someone else makes a mistake, our reputation is shaken.

That night, she wakes up every hour, coughing. The cough catches her throat, grips it, then lets go. We give her some children's medicine to make her sleep. At some point, I lie down beside her in her bed, and when I wake up it is morning.

The day is blustery and cool. On and off, we feel her forehead. Tonight is a friend's birthday, and we will be nine people for dinner. The middle children go next door to babysit for the younger ones. She sleeps upstairs through the noise. When everyone has left, she wakes up, coughing. When I put my arms around her she begins to vomit. Get a bucket, I say to the nearest child. They know the drill. We've been through this countless times, with one or another of them. We have been awakened by children standing by the side of the bed with bloody noses, by a decade of earaches. But now—and we don't know why—we are frightened. She vomits again and again into the bucket, taking rasping breaths. Her forehead is warm but not hot. Her arms flail, and she isn't focusing

We do not have a telephone. The cell phone works only if you walk a quarter mile down Corn Hill to the public-beach parking lot. There are no all-night drugstores. This is why we come here. We like it. We are against the plans for the new Stop & Shop in this small Cape Cod village.

Get Anne, I say. One of the children, white-faced, returns from next door with Anne, who left the table only twenty minutes ago. While we are nonchalant about our children, Anne's father was a doctor in rural South Africa, and knowing more—knowing what can happen—she is careful. When she peers into the bed, she agrees right away that something is wrong: the child looks odd. Her breathing is coming in shudders. Someone remembers that Giulia's grandmother, down the way, has a telephone. No doctor at the Health Services, in Provincetown, is on call for summer residents; we must call the Rescue Squad. We worry that we are being ridiculous, but we call. Her father goes out into the dark to wait for the Rescue Squad.

The van comes in five minutes, red lights flashing. Her temperature is 100.1 degrees, her vital signs are normal. If we are worried we can take her to the hospital in Hyannis, an hour away.

We decide to wait until morning. In the kitchen, she sits on my lap in one of the red chairs. Because we have run out of medicine and have not replaced it during the day—another sign of our foolhardiness, our nonchalance—even though it is too late, we call our friends up the road, Luke and Emily, the parents of our children's friends, and they arrive by car in what seems like an instant, bottle in hand. I take off my vomit-covered sweater. She throws up, just a little, on my shirt. But she is smiling, at Emily, who is looking at her with great tenderness, saying, Poor baby.

The next morning, while the other children sleep, we take her in the station wagon to the health clinic in Provincetown. The waiting room, streaming with light, is almost empty. Two emaciated men sit next to each other on the wall facing the parking lot. There are no appointments until later in the day, but the nurse, after looking at me, comes out to the parking lot to have a look at her. Immediately, there is an appointment. The nurses are beautiful and tall. This is Provincetown, and I wonder briefly if they are transvestites. The doctor's lovely mild face is perplexed. It looks like a virus. Her fever is 101.2 degrees. We are to alternate Tylenol and Motrin every three hours. Her skin is dry to the touch.

At home, she is hungry and wants lunch. She eats ramen noodles, and throws up. The older children wake up, eat breakfast, and are taken to the beach with the surfboards and boogie boards, their horrible pink juice, their box of Goldfish. Her fever disappears.

She wants to play Wiffle ball on the strip of sand on top of our dune. After playing for ten minutes, she goes inside and sleeps with her blanket on the couch. That morning, she vomits twice. In the morning, she got into our bed and, turning her head, vomited directly into my hair. She is hot again. On her back there are a few scattered red marks, as if a bird had walked along the short length of her spine. We call her doctor in New York. He is away, taking his child to college. We speak to another doctor, his partner. He says, "Take her back to Provincetown."

Now at the clinic we are treated as old friends. "Hello, hello," they say.

One of the tall and beautiful nurses takes her blood pressure. The doctor arrives. Her temperature is 102.4 degrees. When she coughs, she takes a moment to catch her breath. Her breathing is shallow, and she is whimpering. The doctor decides to take a blood count: Maybe there is an infection we can't see?

The blood test shows nothing. Her white-blood-cell count is normal. The doctor examines her again. The rash on her back has spread to her stomach: small red dots just under her skin, from sternum to groin. But now she has an infection in her left ear. This is good: there is something to do. New York is called, and agrees with the doctor's recommendation, a massive shot of an antibiotic called ceftriaxone.

It may also attack any bacterial infection that may be lurking. That day's notes say, "case assumed by Dr. Lazarus in New York," followed by the phone number of the pediatrician's West End Avenue office. The antibiotic will be injected into the muscle of her thigh. Her father leaves the room. Hold her legs down, I'm told. I hold her small legs. Are her eyes red? It's hard to tell. She is crying. When we leave the clinic, we are both given get-well stickers. One for Mommy, the nurse says.

In the car back to Truro, past the long seep of dunes where the Pilgrims first found fresh water, I think: scarlet fever. Malaria. Diphtheria. Smallpox. Scurvy. Leeches. Flu? My aunt and my father had polio when they were children. My grandparents closed up their house in Brooklyn and moved to a hotel near the hospital. When we get home, she lies on the couch with her blanket. It's a rainy day, and the hill is full of children. Anna, Lev, and Joseph take turns reading to her. The Wolf eats Grandma; the Troll bellows from under the bridge. She smiles, on and off, and eats a few Goldfish crackers. Her four-year-old friend Adam goes in and out of the house cheerily, checking in. I count up in my head. Taking our children all together, we have thirty-eight years of child-rearing experience. If you include our friends who drop by and stand over the couch like figures in a nineteenth-century print, *The Invalid,* the number lurches up to a hundred and thirty-three. The consensus is that something's wrong with this child. And our friends are not keeping their own children away: the unspoken feeling is that, whatever this is, it isn't contagious. Later I will think, How did we know?

For supper, we have corn from the farm stand, cherrystones and grilled tuna for the grown-ups, and hamburgers for the children. She eats nothing. Asleep in our bed at the back of the house she wakes every half hour and throws up. She asks for water, but it comes right back up. In the morning, she begins vomiting long streaks of bright green bile. When I change her soiled pajamas, which should be soaked because her skin is hot but are not, the rash has melted together into an angry range of welts across her trunk and back.

It is raining again. In the parking lot down the hill, I am on the cell phone to New York. For the first time, I lose my temper when talking to a doctor's office. Told, "The doctor will call you back," I begin to scream into the phone, No, he will not call me back, you will get him, now. I know this is a bad idea. After a long time, the receptionist comes back to the phone. All the doctors are with patients. By now, I am crying. I tell her we have been patients in this practice for a decade, that I've never made such a phone call before, that I know exactly what is going on in the office—there are two kids with ear infections and five kids waiting for school checkups—and she is to get someone right now. Dr. Lazarus comes to the phone.

We return to Provincetown. It sounds to New York that she's lost so much fluid she may need to be hydrated. How will Provincetown know? They'll look at her, they'll know. When we get there, they call an ambulance.

Inside the ambulance, it's our old friends from the Rescue Squad. Should we have taken her to the hospital on Tuesday?

They check her vital signs. This includes pressing her finger until the flesh under the nail turns white, and counting how long it takes for it to flush pink again. It takes too long. She's not getting enough oxygen. Or maybe just enough. Just enough isn't okay. I'm given a choice: either she can hold—or I can hold—a green bear that will breathe pure oxygen into her face or an oxygen mask will be put on over her face. I choose the green bear.

I'm kneeling next to the car seat, on the floor of the ambulance. The green bear starts to work. The technician has a last name—Silva—that's common in Provincetown. Is she a local girl? "You bet I am," she says. "When I was in high school, I couldn't date—everyone was my cousin." She has two kids. Last weekend, the two town ambulances made fourteen trips, a record. Looking down at my own child on the stretcher, I notice two things: the whites of her eyes are bright red, and the fingers on both hands look scorched, as if somewhere along the way she's burned herself.

In the emergency room, the technicians slide her onto a bed. Good-bye, good-bye. I am alone. Her father has followed the ambulance in the station wagon. When he explained in Provincetown he wanted to do this, it became immediately clear that he meant that literally: behind the ambulance, at ambulance speed. He was dissuaded. So he has driven, at a moderately reasonable pace, on the highway, but he's not here yet. A covey of nurses has gathered around her, and they insert an IV into her left hand. She is screaming. Then the ER doctor comes in. He is a man my own age called Nate Rudman— a familiar name. Do I know him? I knew a Seth Rudman in high school, I know a poet called Mark Rudman. Nate comes up blank. She is calming down on the bed. By now I am quite sure I know what is wrong: the little boy next door in New York had been exposed to Coxsackie virus, a minor, irritating, childhood malady. Before we left, it was going around the neighborhood. I am very busy being sure. I am relieved: the proof is her inflamed hands. I inform the doctor, Nate Rudman, that she has Coxsackie virus, but he pays no attention to me. He is gone from the room. The nurses flutter like pigeons. He returns. I tell him again about the boy next door with Coxsackie. No, he says. She does not have Coxsackie. His exact words are: She doesn't have Coxsackie disease. She has Kawasaki disease. It will take two weeks before I can say this properly. Excuse me? This disease, he says, is the primary cause of acquired, potentially fatal, coronary aneurysms in young children.

The blue room turns green. I am standing by the side of the bed. The bed has a bar. I hold on to it. A chair materializes. I sit down on it. Once, when I was a girl, I dove deep from a high bank covered with damp moss into a deep lake, and my mind went blank in the black cold water. I was wearing a Speedo bathing suit. I surface now into the brightly lit room. Before she was born, before we decided to have a child together—she is the first child of our marriage, and the only one—I thought, we are too happy, we are asking the evil eye to come among us. *Kenaharah,* my grandmother would say, if we were too much praised. Don't shine too much light or the Devil will see. The Devil is like a moth—he is attracted to light. When the children are admired, I instinctively deflect it. Pretty is as pretty does, I say. Stop reading twigs in the forest, you idiot Russian, my oldest friend laughs at me. But now it has come to pass.

The doctor, my new friend, my enemy, the bringer of bad news, says, "You need to go to Boston, immediately." He has called Children's Hospital in Boston; we can wait if we like for a confirmation of the diagnosis, but he is sure. "Can you stick out your tongue for me, baby?" he says to her, tiny in the bed. Her tongue is the bright red color of blood. "See," he says to me. "See?" A nurse puts the bar up behind me, so I don't fall out. Now we are both patients. The doctor is speaking to me, and I listen carefully, because I know this is a test. It is the first of a score of explanations we will be given over the next days and weeks, but I don't know that yet. As I listen, I think, This is what growing old is. We think we will learn Sanskrit, learn Greek. Instead, what we learn is more than we ever wanted to know about things we wish we'd never heard of. I think only: You cannot fall apart.

"Kawasaki disease," Dr. Rudman, a total stranger, says, "was discovered by a Japanese doctor. No one knows what causes it; it may be an autoimmune disease that reacts to staphylococcus bacteria. If it is not treated early, within the first ten days, twenty percent of patients, primarily children between the ages of six months and five years old, will suffer heart damage. The aneurysm can be fatal. It can be easy to miss, because the symptoms often do not present themselves at once: the red eyes, the swollen hands, the fever, the rash. The symptoms can come and go."

I lie on the bed holding her hand and think, How dare he talk to me like this? Later, I will realize that he had no choice, that he had to tell me right away so that I would not argue with him, so that I would pay attention, but now I am angry. He tells me what we are going to do: Children's Hospital in Boston is the best place in the world to go, that is where we are going. Arrangements have been made. The treatment is a massive dose of intravenous immunoglobulin. She has had the fever for five days. That is the earliest that Kawasaki disease can be diagnosed. Already, the rash on her hands is fading: once it had disappeared, diagnosis would have been more difficult. In a moment we have gone from being ravaged to being lucky. I realize it is Nate Rudman who has caught it early.

Her father arrives. When she sees him, she throws up. I wipe her face. It's the first time he has seen her on an IV. I am an old hand now, having been here for half an hour. There are four nurses in the room. I ask if it would be possible for them to leave us alone for a minute. I ask him to sit down, and then I tell him.

We sit in the room together for a little while, and then he goes out to make phone calls. Our other children are scattered about; we must have someone collect them. Their grandparents live nearby. They go to our house on the hill and wait for our children to be dropped off by friends. Where are their surfboards, where are their wetsuits?

While he makes calls, I lie on the bed. She is hot but not sweating. I tell her we are going to Boston in another ambulance. Wait until you tell your brother Jack you rode in an ambulance! I say. I tell her the doctors are going to help her get better. They're hurting me, she says. When the nurse looms over to fix the IV, I tell her about our house, how I am a terrible housekeeper, how I am careless when I cook. I am maniacal. I tell her that I never clean properly, that I feed the children chocolate mousse made with raw eggs. She says it is not my fault, ten thousand children could be exposed to some weird thing, and only one will react with Kawasaki. Anyway, no one knows what causes it.

Of course it is my fault.

It will take an hour and fifteen minutes to get to Boston by ambulance. Behind us, cars clot the side of the road. This time the technician is young, overweight, and sweating in his uniform. He is twenty-four years old. I am told to strap myself in on the bench next to the stretcher. Instead, I crouch on the floor, beside her head. She does not let go of my hand. I remind her how when we drove up to the Cape a few weeks ago, our car started to rattle, and we took it to the garage. Remember how it went up in the air, and the little man came to fix it? It was the gasket, she says, nodding solemnly. Her huge blue eyes stand out like anemones against the reddened whites. And then he fixed it and we went to Corn Hill? That's what this is like, I tell her. In the next days, we will talk about the car, and the little man, again and again. And it cost thirty-five dollars! she says with a whisper of glee.

Her hand is hot, her fingers like burning twigs. I hold on to it. I think, If this child dies, I will go mad. I think of a woman who wishes me ill, and I think, If something happens to this child, I will kill her. The technician asks me if I am all right, because I am crying. "If you act upset, you know, it can upset her," he says.

I give him a look of pure malevolence. He is right. He says, "I know how you feel."

"Do you have children?" I ask him.

"No, not yet."

I tell him he is wrong.

He has a girlfriend. She works in Sandwich. He was in a car accident last year and she came every Sunday to see him. The problem is she's always tired.

Drop her, I think. She's twenty-three and she's tired?

It's dark in Boston. In the busy emergency room, the walls are yellow. The nurse is called Mike. The television set is on in the little room. She takes three bites of a turkey sandwich, and immediately vomits. Sheets are brought. I change them myself. Once, then twice. So what's going on here? Mike asks. For the fourth time in as many hours, I recite our recent history: the fever, the rash. He pulls up her hospital gown to look at the rash, which completely covers her trunk. The rash has colonized the scrapes on her knee and on her elbow. (She fell, I think, defensively. She's three, it happens!)

We are waiting for "the Kawasaki team," doctors who are pediatric rheumatologists. No decisions can be made until the Kawasaki team arrives. We are lucky to be here, lucky, lucky, where there is a Kawasaki team. I call Dr. Lazarus in New York. They'll know, he says, they'll know. Her father comes in. He is too big to lie on the bed, so he pulls up a chair next to it. I go out to call the children. I ask each one what they would like to be doing if we were home. Rose wants to go back to Corn Hill to see her Italian friend, Giulia, who is leaving on Sunday. Jack wants to go to the flea market, Anna wants to go to the movies, to see *Blue Crush*. The phone is passed around, these things will be accomplished. Anna, the eldest, gets back on the phone. She's talked to my sister, who is a pediatrician, who has told her the truth. She'll be okay, won't she? Of course she'll be okay, I say.

At eleven thirty, four hours after we arrived in the emergency room in Boston, the Kawasaki team arrives. They are friendly and handsome, a well-matched pair. There is no doubt, they say after examining her, that she has Kawasaki disease, but every indication is that she will be fine. I gather myself up from the bed. You can't tell me that with absolute certainty, can you? I ask. No, they say.

Her father and I are in new territory. I need to go to the very end, to the worst possible outcome, and see where I am. He thinks this is a waste of time.

We are moved upstairs, to a room on the eighth floor. It's an all-purpose floor. Some children breathe on their own, some don't. In the room, we try to sleep but she keeps waking up. She is covered with wires. It hurts when they pull. She was a colicky baby and for three months stopped crying only when I held her. I held her. When can we go home? she asks. I am ashamed of myself even as I think it that I am angry we are missing our time at the beach. It is Friday. We can leave once she has had no fever for twenty-four hours. Before she leaves, she'll have an echocardiogram, to establish the extent of the damage. The nurse comes in every hour. Right now her temperature is 103.5 degrees.

Kawasaki disease is about time and space: it's about measurement. If the coronary arteries expand too far—the difference is in millimeters—the damage is irreversible. There are only thirty-five hundred cases a year in the United States, but it is suspected that more are undiagnosed. It's apparently not contagious. Occasionally, there are geographic clusters, three or four children from the same area, but there's no real evidence. The dose of immunoglobulin retards the expansion of the arteries, and it matters how quickly the child receives the dose. The product has to be mixed. The components are frozen and they have to be defrosted. Her dose is ordered by the Kawasaki team at midnight, but it doesn't appear on the eighth floor until 5 a.m., because for two hours the order sat on someone's desk.

We are so exhausted that, even as wretched as we are, we could probably manage to sleep, but at 3 a.m., the room is rocked with noise. It's a double room, and three feet away, beyond the curtain, someone heavy is hurling himself (herself?) against the wall of a crib. *Bang, bang, bang.* Then a high-pitched keening, with no words. Yelping. In the din, a woman's voice says, "Oh dear, you got up too early, didn't you, didn't you." She croons this. The banging and the growling continue. Holding hands, we hide in the white bed. In this long night, we have plunged, hapless, into a fairy tale. A nurse comes in on the hour to check her vital signs. What is that noise? I ask the nurse. She shakes her head at me, censoriously. The roar continues. A nurse comes in, finally, with immunoglobulin, which replaces the hydration IV pack. The countdown starts. Gray light creeps into the room. At eight, a head peeks around the curtain. It belongs to the night crooner: a pale, dumpy woman with short, dyed-red hair. She is wearing a Red Sox sweatshirt and navy-blue sweatpants. She could be forty, or sixty.

"Did she keep you up?" she asks. There is no word for her

tone but consoling. "She's deaf and blind, you know, so she can't hear herself. I'm sorry if she kept you up."

We look at each other. We have known from the beginning that things could be worse. Here is worse. Sunny, composed, the woman emerges from the bathroom. She says, "I'm going to brush her hair. She loves to have her hair brushed." We listen, and from the other side of the curtain comes the sound of crooning, and what we can just make out as laughter.

A few minutes later, she rounds the curtain again. She is pushing a wheelchair. In the chair is a little girl with gleaming hair. She is wearing a pinafore, pink socks, and white sneakers. Her arms hit out at nothing, and her legs are oddly flaccid. Her ears are too big for her face, and the lobes are pointed. How terrible, I am thinking, to bear such a child.

Her mother looks at her. "She's four. She's adopted," she says to us matter-of-factly. "When she was ten weeks old. Her parents couldn't take it—you know, the problems. They're wealthy, in California." She pauses, stroking her hair. "Sometimes he sends me money. I send him pictures, but I have to mail them to his office. The mother—she can't stand to look at them." She looks at us fiercely. "Their own flesh and blood."

Then she's benign again. "We live in New Hampshire, but we're here a lot. Cyclical vomiting. But I think we're going home today." She unbuckles her from the wheelchair and takes her by two hands, like a toddler.

"Look who's walking," cries a nurse in the reception area. There's a muffled sound of applause. Our own child, in bed but awake, looks after her. "That girl is like me," she says. We look at her aghast. She points to the IV in her hand. "She has a mitten, too."

A moment later, the same nurse—the nurse who would not speak to me in the early dawn—comes in again. She is all of twenty-five, twenty-eight, Boston Irish. She shakes her head. "There are three more of them at home. She takes care of them with her sister." She pauses, checking the monitor. "I think she's very religious." Later, we will tell our friend Storm, a priest, about the little girl, and we will accuse Storm of sending her to us. For now, we are stunned.

The days blur. Her father goes back to the Cape to take care of the other children, to round up their socks and flip-flops and towels from the houses of friends where they've left them. He drives back to the hospital the next day. We make telephone calls. No one's ever heard of this. Everyone goes on the Net: the phone rings with facts. Her grandmother flies up from New York, and takes up residence in a hotel across the street from the hospital. I become an old hand, I know where the Jell-O is kept down the hall. I do not leave the hospital. The immunoglobulin drips into her arm.

Her temperature drops, and for a few hours she responds. The fog lifts, and in those minutes we can see her, we get our child back. She wants blue Jell-O, she wants red. She wants ice cream. "I think my soup is actually warm," she says. "No, it's actually cold." But three hours after the IV drip stops, her fever almost immediately shoots back up again and she is gone. We have to do it again, says the Kawasaki team, which has become one person, a doctor from Nebraska in a violet sweater who has been in the hospital two days. In one or two percent of the cases we see, she says, this happens. What she actually said, first, was: I don't want to tell you this.

Because I am an idiot—even now!—a person (still!) who

would send her children to school with a cough, I point out that it's early evening, the witching hour: everyone's fever goes up at night. She's cranky and tired. I have four children, I know this. No, the doctor, whose name is Dr. Woodward, says. Her pale face is rigid with sleeplessness. I am sitting on a hard wooden chair, a rocking chair, next to the monitor. By now I am so far, far away from anywhere I have ever been that I barely recognize my own voice asking a question. I know the thing to do is to turn and look directly at the doctor, and I do this. "What happens," I ask, "if the fever doesn't go down this time? What will we do?"

The answer is nothing. There will be nothing to do. They had left the IV tube in her hand after the first dose of immunoglobulin in case they had to do it again. I didn't know that, now I do. Her father is on the way back to the Cape. I wait to call him until he's off the road, but he calls from the car. We decide he will stay with the other children. This time, Dr. Woodward takes the request for the immunoglobulin down to the lab herself. It is mixed quickly: the new dose starts three hours later.

By now, she has had Kawasaki disease for seven days, during which she's been feverish for all but three hours. At night, she and I sleep in the same bed. In the middle of the third night she sits bolt upright in the bed and screams, "Where's my mommy?" The immunoglobulin drips into her arm through the clear tube. Wires cover her chest. Despite the tube, she tries to get out of bed. "I'm looking for my mommy!" she screams. Her body is covered with wires, the fluids leach from the IV into her bandaged hand.

"Don't look at the monitor," the nurses say. "It doesn't mean anything." When it flashes, they run in to check. Four aspirins a day keep her blood from clotting, and I grind them up and put them in her blueberry yogurt. "Just a spoonful of sugar helps the medicine go down," sings Julie Andrews, on the video screen. Everyone passing by looks in and says, "I love *Mary Poppins*."

She has two echocardiograms. Her heart is like a pulsing flower. She lies on her side while I tell her the story of "The Nutcracker Prince." She is coated like a jujube with the blue jelly. We go further and further into the forest. We learn the first findings. The function of her left ventricle is slightly depressed; there is a small pericardial effusion, which means she has fluid around her heart; her aortic root is at the upper limits of what's considered normal, as is her left coronary artery. This is what they would expect to find with acute Kawasaki disease. When I was a little girl, I played every summer on the same beach where my children play now, with the children of my parents' friends. When the phone next rings, it is one of those friends. Now he is a pediatric cardiologist. Listen to me, he says. He sets up appointments—here, there, for when we return to New York. I call Dr. Lazarus in New York. Good, he says. Good. These are the people to see.

The second treatment works. She eats a dish of rice and peas. The nurse comes in every hour and checks her temperature. I become more superstitious than ever. I cross my fingers. Her fever stays down.

We have not been outside the hospital for five days. The night before we leave, another child, a little boy, is admitted with Kawasaki disease. His mother is a nurse. "I called my friend on the way here," she says, "and I said, 'Look it up.' My friend called me right back, and started reading." The mother pauses. She is in tears. "I thought, How can he have something I've never heard of? I had to pull off the road."

I decide to make the homecoming festive, and take the ferry across Cape Cod Bay to Provincetown. Her grandmother accompanies us. The day is warm and windy, and the bay glistens. If her fever goes up even half of one degree, we are to return to the hospital immediately. Over the next days, I will put my hand on her forehead so often she swats me away. Back in New York, she'll see four doctors in three weeks, and the one they all lead to, a large, kind man, the wizard at the very center of the maze, who listens to her heart intently for a full five minutes while she sits absolutely still, as she has learned to do, will say to me, in early October, She's fine. Her left aortic root may be slightly enlarged, but she's fine. Two weeks later, she'll cough while she's eating breakfast and I'll start to shake and have to leave the room.

When the ferry pulls in, the wind stops. Her father brings the other children to meet us at the dock. She has slept on my lap during the ride, and the button on my jacket has made a red mark on her face. The children are horrified: all their anxiety is centered on that one splotch. What did they do to her face? they cry.

There is news right away. The waves are good, the waves are bad. They ate marshmallows. The biggest news is the mouse. They have found an infant mouse, in the grass at Lev and Joseph's house, and Daddy said they could keep it.

"No mice," I say.

I am instantly a pariah.

"You can't tell them they can't have this mouse," their father says.

"What?" I say. We have been down this route before. We have two turtles, two cats, a fish, and four children, and we are not going to have a mouse.

"Wait," he says.

When we arrive on the top of the hill, the door to the cottage is plastered with homemade welcome-home signs. The mouse is in a matchbox. Hairless, pink, it is only a little bigger than a fingernail. They found it the night we went to the hospital, and they have kept it alive by loading a grass stalk with milk and waiting while he sucks it. They have taken it in turn to do this.

Coats

When my friend Joan came to see me I coveted her coat. It was violet, and the snowflakes that had attached themselves to her as she walked through the park were small spangled stars. I coveted Joan's coat because my first reaction, always when I see I coat I admire, is to wish I owned it. When I see a dress, or boots, or a bag, or hat—I may think, I would like to have something like that, and I may even set out to find one, not that thing but something close—but that is because my relationship to dresses and boots and handbags and hats is not tinged with remorse and loss.

It is not only because I am always cold, although that is true. In winter my children need to be convinced to put on overcoats, and once they are outside, they take them off, holding their coats under their arms and sometimes letting a sleeve trail on the ground. In the summer when they were small they begged to eat supper without their shirts on. At night they sleep naked and in the morning there are mounds of their bedclothes on the floor. Implicit in this is that to be hot is to be a person of vitality. When, long ago, we huddled by the fire on the steppes, a person who allowed cold to seep into her bones was a fool. People who feel the cold are always complaining of old-fashioned ailments: they feel drafts under the door, they suffer from rheumatism and neuralgia. When my grandmother was very old, she always wore a knitted white cap, to avoid a cold in her head. Now when I go out, I always wear a hat; and on the bus, I choose my seat carefully to avoid the air that pierces the weather stripping. My books are sodden from where they have fallen into hot steaming tubs; sometimes I have to buy another copy, so that I can find out what happens. My husband, who is almost always too hot—the only time he is cold is when we are at the sea in the summer and he stays in the Atlantic for hours, and then when he comes out blue and shivering, he is surprised and takes short, noisy showers. My eldest daughter, although she goes out without a coat—because it is a sign of weakness to admit to cold when you are young, and she wears a thin shirt in every kind of weather—without fail takes a hot bath when she gets home to warm her bones, but the youngest comes home from school with her anorak bunched up in her backpack, sweat on her brow. Now that she is older she is cold at night in our drafty house: once when I called when I was away she told me that she had worn gloves to bed, and I thought, not for the first time, What kind of mother am I? Like mine, her hands and feet are always cold. Sometimes, even when it is not very cold out but damp, my fingers turn a yellow-green in the cold, from the first knuckle to the tip—when I was a little girl my father would warm my fingers by cupping them in his hands and blowing into them, as if blowing out a candle.

The first coat I remember was made for me by my mother. When I was very small she made almost all of my clothes. The clothes I wore as a child, and that were worn by my playmates and my cousins, were uniform. We wore smocked cot-

chalantly, in the coldest weather), and the leather was embroidered all over with flowers and leafy stems. I never had such a coat. As a student I was too shy. Now I do have a sheepskin coat. I bought it on the Internet, during a time when I was unhappy and had both too much and too little time. It looked a little like one of those coats my friend recalls so fondly, but it was not like those coats: it had a notched collar of dark sheepskin pile, and a band of dark pile around the hem, and a line of horn buttons. When I received the coat in the mail, in a brown-paper package tied with string and fixed, haphazardly, with stamps, it looked like a package that had arrived from the past. When I put it on in front of the mirror on the top floor of our house, the only mirror that does not distort, but because we put it there years ago for the children is set low on the door, so that you have to bend, slightly, to fit your reflection in the glass, I went downstairs and found scissors in a kitchen drawer, and cut off the hem. It was exactly like shearing a sheep. The scissors cut through the skin with a hiss.

I have had that coat now for three years, it is the second sheepskin coat I've owned, and it is the warmest coat I have. When I bought it, it was stiff and old and like the corduroy coat I had as a child. It could almost stand up on its own, a straw man, a Guy Fawkes coat; like the coats my friend recalls so fondly it has a slightly madcap air: when my husband, to whom I was married when the coat arrived in its time capsule and I put it on, saw it, he said— My mind stops. What did he say? If I think, I will remember it, at the risk of remembering other things. Although when we were married my husband often chastised me mildly about my habit of running up bills, on the subject of new coats, of which I have acquired many, he was silent: on the roster of checks and balances that at that time made up our marriage, I was still a few coats short, for a decade ago when we moved into the house where I still live now, it happened that he threw all my coats away.

This house has five floors and huge drafty rooms, and in summer a honeysuckle climbs into the living room through the iron railings, which are shaped like sunbursts, but before we moved into this house, we lived in an apartment that looked down on this house and across to a church that looked, to me, like a church in Prague. For six people there was one proper closet: the apartment had been built at a time when people used wardrobes, great heavy armoires that were packed like trunks for great voyages, with clothes and shoes and overcoats, although often the people who owned them went nowhere. The closet in the hall was long, and part of it was for all purposes inaccessible: the door opened on the "front end" but six feet of the closet stretched beyond the door—it was possible to retrieve something from the back of the closet only by crawling on all fours, with a flashlight. For many years, before we abandoned the apartment, we discussed opening up the closet wall, but as my husband had a particular aversion bordering on mania against sliding doors of any kind—an aversion that has been borne out in this house, as the sliding louvered doors of my closet, painted very pale green, a color called Abingdon Putty, are perpetually coming off their tracks and jamming. But when we lived there we did nothing to the apartment. It fell apart around us. In the summer I moved all the winter coats to the closet's tight back alley, and switched our summer wardrobe of slickers and ancient linen jackets to the front end. In between, often for a day or two, the winter clothes would be strewn around the bedroom, as if a party were going on in the next room, and the guests had left their coats in a mound on the coverlet and chairs; a room full of coats where a couple quarreling or not could sit in a burrow of pelts as if retreating, for those ten minutes, into a dream of intimacy, and in the morning I would find little piles of ashes on the windowsill, from where someone had smoked a cigarette out the window, their breath freezing in the cold and leaving a smudge of smoke on the sash.

I had, by then, a catalogue of coats. When I was a student, and for some time afterward, I did not have a proper coat, or a coat that recalled in one iota the coats I had worn as a child, made of corduroy or worsted wool. In the spring and fall I wore an olive-green suede jacket I had bought at a secondhand store, which was missing the top button. The lining was acetate, peach-colored; in some places the lining was rent and torn under the arms and had separated from the hem in the back. The suede had rubbed off around the buttons and the buttonholes, and at the cuffs. These places were a sad, rusty brown, as if the jacket had been scorched and then doused with water. When it was very cold I exchanged the jacket for an equally old black nylon jacket I'd found left after a party at the apartment of friends who lived off campus: I'd worn it home when it started snowing. Although I'd dutifully inquired, no one had claimed it; it was the kind of apartment in which a stray jacket could have resided for months. Along the seams the black had weathered to pearl, and tufts of feathers, like cotton wool, interlaced the baffled stitches. The linings of the pockets were torn, so that for years in the winter I would find that my keys or spare change had migrated to the back of the coat, and I would have to take it off and shake it in order to pay for a coffee or unlock a door. To me these coats proclaimed that I was uninterested in clothes: I was a vagabond or, better, a tramp, my mind set on other things: *Hold on tight,* I would say to myself, and *They called me the Hyacinth girl,* and *Come in from under the shadow of the red rock.* The impression was entirely false. I cared in my own way desperately about clothes, and it did not occur to me that there were others, too, going around in tattered clothes reciting; the friends I admired and coveted seemed to wear their clothes like ceremonial armor, as tatting made from the cigarette smoke, cocoons from which some had already emerged as butterflies. About my purdah in tatters I was like a novitiate who has given up the world out of fear.

The first coat I coveted as a child was blue. I was five when my parents bought the white house outside the city in which I would grow up with my sister and brother. The house had iron windows with catches that opened with the turn of a crank. My room had a window seat and a closet with a window: it was a house to look out from. For many weeks my mother had looked at houses; this house, she told me, had belonged for thirty years to a man called Mr. MacGregor. The Mac-Gregors had fixed the window cranks, the MacGregors had bought a new boiler! There was a screened porch with a door whose catch stuck. The screen door to the kitchen locked. Mr. MacGregor showed my mother how the radiators needed to be bled.

When we are children our fears are uncontainable, there is no yesterday in which something did not happen. As a little girl, I knew by heart the story of Peter Rabbit who is nearly killed by a farmer because he has disobeyed his mother. I repeated in my mind the story of his mad escape from the assassin who, before the story begins, killed his father and put him in a pie. Running from Mr. McGregor, Peter is caught in a gooseberry net and is snared by the large buttons on his jacket. I was a child who had been brought up in the city. I had no idea what a gooseberry net might be—it was confusing to think of a net to catch berries. But next came a sentence that seemed to me then of great beauty: *It was a blue jacket with brass buttons, quite new.* I immediately wanted such a coat. My mother no longer made my coats; instead, they were handed down to me by an older cousin. Nothing in the bags my mother unpacked remotely resembled a blue coat with brass buttons that had been made for a rabbit. The space inhabited by my mother and me included even then my utter inability to describe to her what it was I wanted. But had the coat saved Peter? By abandoning his coat, by sacrificing it to Mr. McGregor, he had escaped as surely as if he had traded the coat for his life. A fair exchange, it seemed to me, a coat for a rabbit. For after all, in the end Mr. McGregor hung up the little jacket and the shoes for a scarecrow to frighten the blackbirds. From our new house, my father took the train into the city very early in the morning and returned late at night. When I looked out the window from my window seat, my mother was in the garden that had been Mr. MacGregor's, setting out bulbs.

The second coat I coveted had belonged to my father. It was a covert brown cloth stadium coat, lined with brown plush. He had worn this coat when he was in college in New Hampshire, and the belt, which had a leather buckle, was frayed. It hung in the attic closet next to my mother's silk shantung dance dresses. These dresses had watercolor patterns in pinks and blues, and the waists were small. The closet was lined with cedar. Next to the dresses my father's coat was a behemoth, pocked with tiny moth holes. In the left pocket, which was lined with chamois, was an old half-finished tube of lipstick. The case was black Bakelite and the color was Splendor Red. It had been made by Elizabeth Arden. After I finished school and returned to New York I hardly ever stayed again with my mother and father for more than one or two nights, but one of those nights I came down from the attic with a bag into which I had folded the coat and asked my father whether I could have it. My father is a tall, broad-shouldered man. He is a person who takes up space in a room. When I put it on, the frayed belt went twice around my waist and the hem skimmed the floor.

I retired the black baffled coat. Each time I had been moved to wash it the dye had further bled. In many places it was no longer black but the color of smoke. I wore my father's coat for a series of winters, to the large office building where I worked at a magazine, and I wrapped it tightly around me while I waited for whomever I was going out to lunch with to finish a cigarette in the shadow of the building where we were pro-tected from the wind, and I wore it to parties where I left it in the pile of coats in a distant bedroom of huge apartments that belonged to people who were decades older than I was, whose medicine cabinets were filled with dried-up bottles of Mercu-rochrome and vials of tranquilizers. When, instead, there was a rented coatrack in the hall, I would carefully put my coat on the floor, rolled up and behind the tote bags of editors who were bringing galleys home to read on the train. It seems clear to me now that no one would have stolen my coat or mistaken it for their own, but I was wary. Much later, when I began to have parties in the apartment with the long hall, when I went into the bedroom to make sure that no one had left a cigarette smoking on the windowsill, I would notice furtive signs that reminded me of my own—a jacket tucked carefully into the corner behind the bookcase, a bag hidden behind the armchair pushed against the wall.

In that apartment, by the time I began to shift the winter and summer things in the closet it was usually either too hot or too cold. Winter jackets had been pulled to the fore and crammed between the summer things, or the reverse. I often found crumpled juice boxes in the boots, and cheap toys that had been given to the children as favors at birthday parties which I'd stuffed into the closet, planning to throw them out after they'd gone to bed. These toys were usually in paper bags that also held candy which had turned white and was smeared with mold. The mold in the boots and the forgotten candy were no one's fault but my own. It wasn't remotely possible that anyone but me would clean out the closet.

At the time, I had a dozen coats. These coats included the first coats I had bought, and the last one, which had been bought for me. My father's coat, with its fraying hem, was among them. I found it impossible to give it away to the annual thrift shop drive at the school the children attended. This thrift shop opened for one week a year, in the basement of Synod Hall. The school was on the grounds of the Cathedral of St. John the Divine, and the years the children were there transpired in an atmosphere of damp stone and crying peacocks. I usually worked at the thrift shop, which was part of a fair on the close—there was a bake sale, and a plant sale, and children ran around and squirted water pistols—and for weeks before I sorted through the children's clothes and brought over large shopping bags of outgrown party shoes and snowsuits. At the shop I liked sorting through the bags other people brought. In those years the shop was a kind of clothes swap—months afterward at a party I would find that I was wearing the hostess's Japanese skirt, which she'd given to the thrift shop; at a piano recital another mother was wearing a jacket with purple buttons I'd had made for me in the early 1980s. I had even acquired one of my coats there: a blue cape with a funnel hood.

The first coats I bought were in Venice, and I bought them on the same day. I had just been married for the first time. My husband and I had expected to begin our trip in Rome, but we had spent almost a week, unexpectedly, in Sperlonga, a seaside town between Rome and Naples. When we decided to leave Sperlonga, and pick up our trip, as we had intended, Rome—where we had originally meant to stay in a friend's apartment—had become for various reasons insupportable, and we went instead to Venice.

It was chilly in Venice. Our hotel was next to the opera house, and the voices of singers hung in the cold air of Piazza San Marco. At night a fog curtain closed over the lagoon. I had brought my green suede jacket. The lining by then had deteriorated to a fretwork of peach satin in the seams. We walked all day, and in the late afternoon, when my fingertips had turned white and then yellow, I would return to the hotel and, turning on the tap full blast, lower myself as best as I could into the hip bath in the tiny bathroom in order to get warm. My husband had not been to Venice before. While I was in the tub he would be out, drawing. In the tub I read *The*

Golden Bowl. One afternoon when it was warmer, rather than retreat to the tub after my husband had departed to draw and smoke cheroots on the Accademia Bridge, I found myself staring into a shop window lined with pale leather handbags in ice-cream colors. Toward the back of the shop I could see a rack of coats. Inside, the lights illuminating the glass shelves in the window lit up their beveled edges. The coats were black, brown, crimson, and loden green. The store was deserted. Perhaps the shop girl was having a coffee in the back? If she had been visible, eager to help, I probably would not have gone in and tried on a coat, but alone I felt emboldened, a child playing dress-up. The lines of the coat I put on were nineteenth century. It had rounded lapels, a wasp-waist accomplished by back darts, a bell-shaped skirt, and a single row of embossed pewter buttons that reached the hem, which was ankle length. The sleeves were full but cinched at the wrists with matching buttons. The buttons said "Fendi." The general effect was equestrian. Perhaps because I had recently left behind in Sperlonga the pair of gold and coral earrings that I had not bought, although I now pined for them, a week later, with a kind of desperation (I'd even written to ask if they were still in the shop), I wouldn't have thought of buying it.

I stood for a long time looking into the mirror, in a kind of dream; it was the kind of dream, as the years went on, I know now, in which most of my decisions occur, as if my life were a cloth in which I had missed essential parts of the pattern that I was filling in stitch by stitch, like Penelope. I could not afford the coat, even at the very reduced price (*seventy-five percent off!*). I did think about whether my husband would like the coat: he would, I thought. For a number of years I had been wearing almost exclusively silk and cotton crocheted dresses—garments that many years later had a second life by appearing regularly in Shakespeare productions put on by children. (I spent so much time in the shop that sold those dresses, drinking sauterne with the owner, Margot, that my husband had adopted one of her daughters, who was called Violet, as a model, and had begun to take an interest in the colors the clothes were dyed; the dyeing which took place in the back. Later, Margot's husband, who did the dye lots, tried to run her over with a tractor, on a place they had upstate, and the shop closed.) My husband liked the dresses, although many people did not. He would like the coat, I thought. While I was trying it on, a girl had appeared. She was a tall girl, with very high-heeled black patent-leather boots and matching hair—she stood, slightly bored, by the cash register. When I felt I had looked at myself long enough I asked her about the boots on the floor. I wanted someone to talk to. They too were *seventy-five percent off.* Only a few days before I had refused to buy a pair of earrings that were roughly one fiftieth the cost of the coat. I realized I didn't want her to know how much I wanted the coat—I wanted her to think I bought coats every day of the week, at the drop of a hat. In the moment, convincing the shop girl, whose patent-leather hair, I could now see, was threaded with red glitter, of this entirely untrue fact was of utmost importance. I was wearing the coat—a garment from which it was clear to me I would never be parted.

In order to sit down and try on the boots I had to sweep the voluminous skirt of the coat to the side. There was only one pair of boots in my size. The soft leather was the color of cognac, and the top of the boot, which stopped a few inches above the ankle, was scalloped. I have had those boots now for over a quarter of a century. The leather of the shoe has almost completely disintegrated, and where the leather meets the soles, there are holes that the shoemaker (to whom I have taken the boots countless times) has finally despaired, and encouraged me, with the air of a sister of mercy, to throw them out. Then, without looking at the price, I put the boots on the counter for the girl, who was beginning now to show interest: perhaps I would like to see something else?

No, I was finished. Could I wear the coat out? The girl cautioned me that the coat was not returnable: *ricevuto di ritorno.* I spread my fingers in a mock gesture of supplication: what the gods had willed was not mine to choose. She raised her eyebrows. And what, we seemed to say to each other, could be returned anyway? The girl folded my old suede jacket and put it in the bag with the boots—I was tempted to give it to her. Outside the shop it was colder. Damp was beginning to seep out of the stones. I walked back to the hotel by the opera house, which was quiet now in the late afternoon, and when I got there I took off the coat, hung it up in the wardrobe, a black affair trimmed with gold leaf and a picture of a pagoda under a lotus, lay down on the bed, and went to sleep.

When I woke up an hour later my husband had returned. He was sitting in a chair by the bed, wearing his anorak, and he was drawing me. "Don't move," he said. I stayed as I was for a moment, on my back with my right hand flung over my head and my left leg bent. Then I stretched. "I found something for you," he said. He had come in so recently that his beard was still beaded with water. He looked like Neptune—he often looked like Neptune. When I think of him now, of those years, for I still often see him—after all we were together for almost a decade and have a daughter together, although we parted soon afterward—I imagine him at a distance, as if he were always either walking toward me or away from me. When he painted he held the brush between his teeth. We were both subject to fits of anger and discouragement, but then nothing of married life had happened between us. He was visibly pleased by what he had found for me, and when he suggested that we could go look at it I was happy to go. You can't have it now, he said.

I had woken in a paroxysm of guilt. The long coat, unbuttoned, hid in the closet. I put on my old jacket, which wasn't warm enough, and we walked through the hotel's red lobby into the streets, now lit up like electric eels against the dark. We passed a wine bar we had liked the day before, and a few paces beyond it, in a cul-de-sac, was a shop. The doors were closed and locked, but the windows were illuminated: in one arched window was a hip-length suede coat. The suede was the color of pale cocoa, and the shoulders and button placket were outlined in thin bands of chocolate leather. Reflected in the plate glass, my tattered suede jacket was superimposed on the coat. At the back of the house by the cove where as a girl I went with my mother and father in the summer, there was a cellar door you could stand on. It was painted copper, with rust-resistant paint, and even in the morning, the metal was hot on my bare callused feet. There weren't any mirrors in the house, except for the medicine cabinet over the sink. If you stood on the door, you could see yourself in the kitchen casement window. When we returned after almost a year away, I would stand on the door and look. Behind me were the pine trees, their green needles ending in spikes that matched the cellar door, as if they'd been singed. I would scrutinize my reflection, which came back to me neatly divided into quadrants. Had I grown? I had no idea of what I looked like. I saw a middle-sized girl, slightly round in ways she found detestable, with a furrow between her brows, squinting.

My taller reflection on the shop window wavered. There was condensation on the glass. My husband drew an X with his finger. "There's your coat," he said. He had seen it earlier this afternoon. They were holding it. I could try it on in the morning. He would have bought it but had wanted to make sure it fit. I burst into tears. *How could I have not known?* In the shop, trying on the coat I had bought, with its snake of buttons and swashbuckling skirt, how could I have not known that a few blocks away, perhaps at that very moment, my husband had found a coat for me? A chasm opened. At the bottom I could see coats piled willy-nilly: beautiful coats, fur coats, tattered coats. When I was eight years old, I was in love with my best friend, Joanne, who lived a few minutes' walk from my house on a street called Beach Drive. "Beach Drive" I used to like to say to myself. Where was the sea? The street led nowhere near the sea. We played almost every day at her house or at mine. At her house we were often joined on the swing set by Gus, who lived next door, who was a dwarf. He was older than we were, but he was smaller. He was kind, and he knew everything. He was, my friend Joanne said, "a font of wisdom." Gus knew how far we were from the sun, and when the sun was likely to burn out and leave us in cold and darkness. Sometimes we played at cold and darkness. We draped an old tarp over a bush. If it was winter, we took off our coats. It was important, Gus told us, to feel the cold. His birthday was on leap year: although he was twelve, he was really only three years old. There was no end, I was learning, to conundrums. My children have grown up in New York City in apocryphal times—after the Twin Towers exploded we began to worry immediately, when the children left for school, or when we went to the store or to work, whether we would ever see each other again, a worry that took root and grew leaves in every cell of our bodies. If you took apart our veins you would see the snake eyes of those shoots whose tendrils have rooted us to a spot of fear, colonized by small, skittering wild life. Because of this our children do not take the bus or the subway or walk anywhere alone until they are old enough to walk away, without us.

Joanne and I were allowed to walk each other halfway home, a distance of about an eighth of a mile. When we walked we talked nonstop. When we got to the midpoint, we often turned back and started again. Often we did this so many times that her mother would call my mother, wondering where we were. Then one of our mothers, annoyed and wiping her hands, would appear and divide us. It was late. We had homework. We needed to eat. I walked home with my mother, wearing my navy-blue wool coat. My mother is five feet one inch tall. Gus, who knew everything, had told me that soon I would be taller than my mother, a fact I turned over in my mind. In my family now our eldest daughter is the smallest, which irritates her, as if her power as the eldest is somehow diminished. When some children came by our rickety house last summer they were amazed. How could it be? Magic. I thought of Gus, who by the time he was five, or twenty, was dead. In the meantime he had grown wizened and hunched, even smaller. I went less frequently to Joanne's house (a new girl she liked better played there more often) and I rarely saw Gus. He had begun to make me feel uncomfortable: he was a know-it-all, I thought. My own body was becoming less familiar to me. When I looked in the mirror I focused, in turn, on my nose (was it a different color than the rest of my face?) and my mouth (my gums were too prominent). I read fairy tales, and in each one the troll who asked questions or demanded recompense had Gus's face. *But it was you who had the answers,* I would accuse the face, silently.

In the bookcase behind the piano in Joanne's house was a volume of black-and-white photographs that looked wet to the touch. A roomful of shoes. Another of coats. A convoy of trucks. Barbed wire. Some chickens pecking at a semicircle of dirt. We rationed these images, but it was important to look at them. The rule was we had to look at each one before we could turn to the center page. It was the only photograph that spanned two pages, and it was bisected by four stitches of pale thread. This was the actual book binding, we thought, what held the book together. If we cut the thread, well, the book would fall apart, wouldn't it? We didn't cut the thread, just tested it. Our fingers were small and we could worm an index finger under the thread and give it a try. One place where we had done this a number of times was loose and a little gray. We huddled on the window bench, our white legs curled up under us. It was the 1960s, little girls didn't wear trousers to school. Joanne's thick hair was the color of corn. She wasn't made to wash it as often as I did. My hair was straight and black and fell halfway down my back, but I couldn't sit on it. Joanne could sit on her hair. It was the aspiration of my life, at eight, to sit on mine. I am digressing, because even now it is hard to look at the photograph. Who could? Why were we expected to look? The truth is we weren't expected to look, but there it was, on the bookcase. The rule was—what was the rule? That rule was that we had to look until the count of ten. We took turns, counting. Was it the first time I saw fish piled on a dock in the seaside town where I spent the summer with my mother and father that I thought of the photograph?

Or did I see the fish first? The bodies looked like coats, one inside the other.

After we looked at the picture we would lie under the piano, and pretend to be coats, one inside the other, one over the other. The smell of the rug in the living room was animal. I traced the salmon-colored wool triangles with my finger. Then, we called adults by their last name: Mrs. This, and Mrs. That. Joanne's mother was the only adult I knew who had told me to call her by her first name. Hello, Mary, I said. Good-bye, Mary. Thank you, Mary, for having me. Mary had told me the pattern of the rug was called "Tree of Life." Once, under the shrubs with Gus, after the sun had gone out, I drew the tree of life with a stick in the ground. Our coats were off. Show me what you do, he said.

D
o you like it? my husband asked. I did like it, I said. He looked at the door of the shop. It would be open at eleven o'clock in the morning. Then we went to the wine bar and when I started to cry again—I cried a lot in those days, I didn't have children yet, to whom I would say as my grandmother had said to me, "Save your tears." "For what?" my elder daughter would ask, who cried then as she does now

in great, windy gusts, as if a storm has taken her. Then I cried
what I later would call floods, tears I mark with my daughters
by tracing the tracks of tears, like snails, running down our
cheeks, tears laced with mockery, what my own mother called
crocodile tears. *In that contre . . . ben gret plntee of Cokarilles.
Theise Seprentes slen men, and thei eten hem wepynte,* wrote Sir John
Mandeville in his travel journal, *Voyage and Travailes,* in 1372,
buried under the epigraph, "rich only in memory, he settled
after seeing much for a small continent." In the bar I drew a
coat on a napkin, a coat like the ones I had worn as a child,
with its crocodile of buttons and velvet collar.

In the end, I left Venice with both coats. When we returned
to the hotel I opened the enormous wardrobe and modeled
for my husband the coat I had bought that afternoon. Turn
around, he said. He especially liked the little belt in the back,
which I had not noticed. In the morning without discussing it
we returned to the shop, a store where I would later, in New
York, at its Madison Avenue outpost, buy extremely expensive
wallets although I had almost no money to put in them, wallets which looked as if they had been woven from vellum, all
of which were stolen within months of purchase, and bought
the other coat. When we left Venice, it was thirty degrees
colder than it had been in Sperlonga, but I was warm. In New
York a few weeks later, I received a postcard from our friend:
she had been swimming—in October! No husband! No earrings! She had bought a new bathing suit!

I wore both coats for years. I wore them, as my great-aunts
would have said, and did say, *into the ground.* In time the two
coats were joined by others. From the store where my husband
sat and drew Violet, I fell in love with two more: one in purple

wool, knitted into a shape like a tulip, and another made of mohair in which I looked like an owl. I wore the coats when the children were small—by that time my husband and I had a child, and then parted, and the second man I married had two small children, and the smallest children pulled at the buttons that said Fendi but which were sewn on so well they never came off. In time the suede coat my first husband had found in the window of the shop in San Marco collided with a platter of just-roasted chickens, in the market where I went almost every day with the children, to shop for pasta and diapers and juice. There was a stain the shape of Africa on the sleeve, and when I sent it to be cleaned, it returned stripped of its glow, like the saltimbanques by Picasso, the faces scrubbed like potatoes, that just yesterday my daughter, now eighteen and trained in how to look by her father, stood in front of at the museum, and after an hour of barely speaking to me or to anyone, let out a groan. "Look what they've done!"

In the long closet I hung up coats I bought: the Japanese cape from the school thrift sale; a pink jacket from Paris I had convinced my mother to buy and which she had almost immediately given to me; my father's coat, thick with grime at the hem; a fake fur coat that looked like no animal that had ever lived, and under which I carried my youngest child in the park, along the river, all the fall and winter after she was born. In a shop, when she was small, when I was momentarily disenchanted with being anyone's mother, anyone's at all— a shop on Eighty-first Street that sold other people's castoffs or things they had bought and couldn't afford—I tried on a narrow black leather double-breasted coat which skimmed my knees. It was less than the coat had been a decade ago (*seventy-five percent off*) but now those dollars directly translated in my mind into school fees and the light bill and new socks and chopped meat.

I went home and pined for the coat. There was no reason for this. I had many coats. I told myself I wasn't cold: indeed, I had more coats than any person needed to have. It was winter in New York, and on the street corner near the building where we lived then, there was an outsize box from the Salvation Army, overflowing with coats discarded by those who didn't hoard their clothes but gave them away. There was nothing I needed. Nevertheless, I thought about the black leather coat. I drew it on a napkin. By the third day the price of the coat reduced itself in my mind. By sleight of hand, a honed agility in which one hand does not know what the other is doing, I calculated that it was worse to spend so much time pining for the coat, which was, after all, a material object, than to buy it and be done with it. I was in the midst of the years in which I didn't know that desire is infinitely replaceable. I called the shop and asked the girl if she could put the coat aside for me: I would pay for it over the phone and pick it up later in the week. I described the coat, she went to look. It was gone. For a few weeks the image of the coat hung before me, then turned ghostly and vanished, only to be resurrected a month later: the coat was gone because my husband had taken the picture I had drawn on the napkin to the shop. He had bought the coat. He had wrapped it in tissue paper, and kept silent when I mourned the loss of the coat which had not and now would never be mine.

When the first pinprick of something going awry touches our skin it is often so light, so benign, that in an instant it is gone. "Button up your overcoat," I sang to the children, as my mother sang to me. "Take good care of yourself, you belong to me." The wind comes up. Why could I not have what I wanted but it had to be given to me, instead?

I've worn the coat for many years. It is the coat I take with me when I travel. The black leather is turning silvery at the seams. When we moved from the house with the long serpentine closet in which you had to search on your hands and knees for a familiar hem to a house with ten closets with tall doors that we bought from a building next to ours which was being torn down (we liked to tell people the house we built inside the shell was built around the doors, as if someone was always coming or going, which turned out, in that house, to be true), I packed all my coats—the long green coat I had bought in Venice, with my then husband, and its companion, now stained almost beyond wearing, and the navy-blue Japanese cape, and the indeterminate fur coat in which I'd carried my last baby like a papoose, and sung her the overcoat song, and the song about Georgie Porgie, and the boy in the Milne poem who lets his mother go down to the end of the town, in Riverside Park with bright leaves and then snow on the trees, and my father's coat, and my mother's pink jacket, into bags, where they lay one inside each other, and moved them into the basement next to the coat closet in the mudroom. It was summer by then, and I had no time to unpack them, and when I looked for them the morning of the third day of our move, they were gone. My husband had mistaken the bags for trash. All but the leather coat, which I had thrown over a chair upstairs, in the big echoing house with its long interior views, in order to feel at home.

For a few days I called trash companies to see if there was a way I might find the coats. A fool's errand. At night I was overcome with remorse, and at the same time I was disgusted with myself, crying for coats. The children were well, after all. We were happy. It was a new chapter: What did I need with my old coats? I pictured my coats with their arms around each other, on a heap of trash, on a barge going out to sea. A ludicrous image.

I now have other coats—a raincoat with an allover pattern of purple pansies, the second shearling, with its notched collar. Over the years my second husband bought me a pale coat cut almost on the lines of the coat I first bought in Venice, a coat so beautiful that people stop me in the street when I wear it, which is almost never. The last Christmas we lived together, I bought him a coat: a thick gray worsted coat, with a hood. Button up your overcoat, don't step on hornet's nests, one if by land, two if by sea! When Dido arrived in Carthage, she asked, in exchange for gold, for all the treasure she could put inside the skin of a bull. When they gave her the skin she cut it into tiny pieces and placed them in a semicircle that enclosed the city. When I was a child, like my children I was always hot, and now I wear a sweater at the seaside even in summer. When we sat under the hedge with Gus, who was both older and younger than we were, and now that we are older and he is dead, is always younger, the chill mounted as we drew stick figures in the ground with twigs, our stiff coats next to us in the dirt, waiting for it to get really cold. My children hand their coats made of feathers back and forth, they leave them at school, they forget them.

When the children were small they read a book I had read

as a child about a little bear who is cold. Each time he comes to the door he tells his mother, "I am cold, I need something to put on." His mother gives him mittens, a hat, a coat. At the end, he is still cold and she says, "But little bear, you have a fur coat!" And he takes off his hat and gloves and coat and goes out to play in the snow. Now, I too have a fur coat. It belonged to a friend, who gave it to me when she was given a new one. She called and said: "Do you want this? You are always cold." When she called I was sitting in our drafty house, in front of a space heater. The coat was remodeled to fit me. When I went to the furrier in order to have this done he said, "What do you want to spend?" and I said, "The price of a good cloth coat."

Restaurants

Some restaurant stories are tales of the lost world. On the corner of 116th Street and Broadway, now, is a Chinese restaurant called Ollie's to which one of my daughters, since she was very small, has gone to so often with her father that the proprietor, a blade-thin man whose high cheekbones are two half-moons in his worried face, brings her scallion pancakes as soon as she sits down. She is seventeen now; she has eaten there, conservatively, thirty times a year since she was two. For a very long time it was the only place she went out to eat: it's her proto-restaurant. But to me Ollie's is on the corner where an old Chock full o'Nuts used to be. The other day I was headed down into the subway on that corner when my phone rang—it was an old friend who was born in Manhattan, twenty blocks away, but who has lived in the country for years (in New York, anything beyond a commuter rail is the country, but he lives in real country, roads with nothing on them but trees) and when he calls he always asks where I am: the city is still, for him, the grid of his heart, and I said I was by the old Chock full o'Nuts. Or I could have said, where T—— used to live. Ollie's means nothing to him.

Like most New York restaurants, Ollie's is on the ground floor of an apartment house—twenty-five years ago, he lived for a time in that building on the fifth floor. It was a borrowed apartment (borrowed from T——); in those days, apartments were sublet and borrowed more casually: they were mainly rented, not owned, and at least in that neighborhood, near Columbia, they passed from hand to hand. All I can remember of the interior is a black leather sofa and a red dressing gown hanging on the hook in the bathroom. T—— ended up marrying the girl I once found, unexpectedly, on that sofa. Once in a while we bought coffee at the Chock full o'Nuts, and whenever I see Edward Hopper's picture *Nighthawks,* I think of that coffee shop. Even during the day, it had that brooding, hopeless quality, of conversations not started because, even if she said something, there was nothing to say. Very early in the morning, the harsh smell of the coffee coiled itself into that apartment and slowly browned the old copies of *Newsweek* and the *Asia Times.*

In those days I never ate at home. We certainly never cooked at T——'s. We went to the Knickerbocker, down on University Place, or a restaurant whose name I've forgotten at One Fifth Avenue, or to the Blue Bar at the Algonquin, where we pretended it was 1945. There was a restaurant we liked on Seventy-second Street above a flower stall where we always ordered the butterflied pan-roasted chicken breast, something I've never eaten or made since, and a French restaurant on Broadway which has had a dozen incarnations since then: it's one of those haunted New York corners where restaurants cannot flourish, a culinary Bermuda Triangle, and any ship that pulls up there capsizes, with no survivors. Sometimes we went to the Indian restaurants down on Sixth Street that my daughter has recently discovered; they're still there, just a little more expensive, the smell of cumin and curry wafting up through the grates. One of those restaurants was supposedly better than the others, but the joke was that it was all the same kitchen, smoking down under First Avenue in a cul-de-sac of the subway, that subterranean landscape where any kind of enterprise flourished. You could get your shoes shined and buy a bunch of roses, and you still can.

The first great restaurant-going epoch of my life was in 1963, when I ate once a week with my parents in a Chinese restaurant in Manhattan near the 125th Street IRT overpass. I was about four. Because soon after that my sister and brother were born, we moved out of the city and became a family that almost never ate out (the economics of this were opaque to me then), that cramped restaurant, in its halo of fragrant steam, the Day-Glo ducks hanging in the window, remained with me. Eating out was in its way more private than eating at home, where even the chairs knew you. That it was the last moment I had my parents' attention to myself is a thought that has only recently occurred to me. I always ordered the same thing: ten different ingredient soup. Tiny shrimp, slivers of chicken, and shreds of orange pork floated in the magic broth, along with tiny white squares of—what? It was more than a decade before I saw it again, floating in a particularly gruesome meal at the college co-op, where good cooking meant tossing every bit of refuse into a stockpot that simmered endlessly on the stove: *tofu*. After that, it was like looking up a word in the dictionary—bean curd, at least in Cambridge in the seventies, turned up everywhere. But there was a Spanish restaurant, on Boylston Street, where I was taught how to eat black squid in ink sauce, and prawns . . . That restaurant is closed too, and the street has another name.

It came as a surprise to me when I discovered that there were families who went out to dinner as a matter of course. When I was in college I knew a boy whose family went to a Howard Johnson in Westfield, New Jersey, for pancakes every Sunday night, and a girl to whom Sunday night supper meant eating with her grandparents at Lutèce. One girl I knew always celebrated Thanksgiving at Patsy's, an Italian restaurant in the theater district. Other families had other rituals. Recently a friend told me a tale of exotica. When her mother was a little girl she and her sisters were sent for the summer to a sleepaway camp in Maine. Before they left, they were taken to dinner at the St. Regis Hotel. On their return, nine weeks later, they were picked up at Grand Central Station, driven back to the St. Regis, deposited in the tub and scrubbed, and room service was ordered. It was spaghetti, which they were not allowed to eat at home. Suffice it to say my own childhood experiences do not equal this. Once a year, my mother took me shopping with her. In those days, the dressing rooms were mirrored on two sides, and you could see yourself reflected smaller and smaller, diminishing into the silver distance. I looked to myself like a fish, white and unappetizing in the glass. Afterward, a treat, I was allowed to order a mint chocolate chip ice cream soda at the lunch counter at Bonwit Teller. I can still feel the taste of that green froth, slightly medicinal on my tongue.

The other day, it was the last day of school for my youngest daughter, and we had listened to the bell ringers and the songs—"Over the Rainbow" and "Ukrainian Folk Tune." The girls were magically transformed from fifth into sixth graders, pinching themselves to see if they felt any different, and the older girls, stricken with tears, graduated from Middle to Upper School, already dragooned by the idea of loss. We had arranged as usual to have a celebratory lunch with her friend Ellen, and her mother, who as it happens had been a girl at that same school, so there was the feeling of the past being present, and the girls as somehow doubling us. The sister who ate every week at the Chinese restaurant had graduated the year before from that same school, so as I watched the girls file out, she was there too, at every age except the one she is now, in my mind, crossing that stage and the podium.

We usually went with the girls to a restaurant called Quatorze Bis, on the north side of Seventy-ninth Street. It was satisfyingly far from school, four long blocks, far enough to feel that you had left the school's force field but close enough to walk. When my daughter was very small, all she would order in a restaurant was pasta with butter, but more recently she will order an omelet with mushrooms, or roast chicken, and eat happily. If she could, she would order mashed potatoes on the side. The waiters were ceremonious with the little girls. Quatorze had on the menu things that she liked and recognized, and served profiteroles the size of spaceships, and the mothers, grown up, could have a glass of white wine and congratulate each other on another year in which the children had done well in school, and practiced their volleyball skills and learned the provinces of Canada, and we had muddled through. That year, I think, I had a broken heart.

But this year when we left the school it was hot. It had been crowded in the lobby. One backpack had been lost, then found. The girls were in their special-day dresses, not uniforms, as befit Last Day, and they were pulling at the elastic on the unfamiliar shoulder straps of their sundresses. Suddenly Quatorze seemed too far to walk on the hot pavement. We suggested the Mansion, around the corner, what passes in New York for a diner, and used to be called a luncheonette, where they could get pancakes. Nothing appealed. The feeling of celebration petered out. Wistfully, one of the girls said, *I wish we could go swimming.*

It turned out we could. At our friends' apartment three short blocks away bathing suits were unearthed. The week before, my friend had joined a club where the children could play tennis. Her parents had belonged to this club, and she had gone there as a child; in the welter of the last days of school— because she also taught at the school, and had another child, who was also finishing school that week—she had forgotten she had joined. We waited while the dog was fussed over and fed and left barking in the apartment, and then took a taxi. We emerged on the East Side near the river in the Fifties, in a neighborhood remote from my map of the city. I had been taken there as a child to visit an elderly family connection. The door to a cavernous echoing apartment was opened by a uniformed maid, and the rooms were filled with objects that seemed even to me then to be preordained: there had been no choice but these lamps, these rugs and armchairs, which had been rooted to the spot for fifty years. The last time I had been to the neighborhood, silent as a grave, was for the reception after a memorial service for an art dealer and collector known for his eye and his irascibility, whom my husband had befriended. He had a young wife whose mascara ran, and three sharp middle-aged daughters, the reverse of a fairy tale.

When we got out of the cab with the two girls, the silent

street was hot as a bread oven. Each building had a funereal black or green awning shading a brass or gold door. Although we were almost at the river it was impossible to have any sense of it, for the street was that unusual thing in New York, a dead end, all sight of the highway cut off by a high wall at the end, which now bisected the residential neighborhood from the gulls and barges. We passed from the dream of heat into a door marked ———, and the clock went back forty years. There was the board in which members were "in" or "out," the old red carpet never replaced, the ladies' room with the carefully folded hand towels and bowl for change. There was a moment of panic when my daughter thought she had left off the bottom of her borrowed bathing suit, but there it was, on her bottom, under her sundress, which was printed with sailboats.

It was too early to swim: it was "adult time" in the pool, which was indoors, and had glass windows with huge casements facing a sunken garden, so that it looked and felt like an aquarium. An elderly couple were paddling, wearing bathing caps. The place was absolutely still. There were a few gliders, covered with plastic cushions printed with flowers. The cushions smelled of damp, and Lysol, and something else indefinable—mold, or the indrawn breath of a different era. The girls were starving. I think, said my friend, there's food. There was a telephone on a stand. It was a black phone with a handle and a dial, of the kind you hardly ever see anymore. She picked up the receiver, and in a moment, apparently, there was a voice at the other end. This is Mrs. ———, she said, and I'd like to order some lunch. Then she nodded and put down the phone. After a long moment in which nothing happened at all, in a hush broken only by the sound of slow paddling from the pool, a waiter in black trousers and a mustard-colored double-breasted jacket glided out of a door at the far end of the room, holding a gigantic menu. The girls pored over it. They would have, they said, BLTs and lemonade. Order dessert now, we urged, and then it can come *at the same time.* I think we both felt that the waiter was an apparition, and we could not count on him, like the ghost of Hamlet's father, appearing often again. The choices were ice cream or Nesselrode pie, and since we could not come up with an explanation of the latter—I had a vague idea of creaminess but had not seen it on a menu for decades—they chose ice cream. The waiter bowed to the girls, a gesture they had not seen before, and vanished, nodding.

After an interminable time, during which the girls played hangman on a crumpled napkin I found in my handbag, the waiter reappeared. He was pushing a small silver cart with tiny wheels, and on the cart was a small Byzantine city of silver domes. The girls sat up straighter at the table. With another bow, he whisked the plates off the cart, placed them in front of them, and whisked off the domes. Underneath were their sandwiches, three slices of white bread each, with the crusts cut off, festooned with toothpicks decorated with tiny streamers of green, yellow, and red cellophane. On the side were some tiny cornichons, which my daughter loves. Next to the plates were two smaller covered silver domes, shiny with cold. Beneath them were two scoops of the chocolate ice cream of my childhood—pale, faintly crystallized at the edges, in a just melted lake of paler cream.

Because it was Last Day and since *everything had come at the same time* and *the ice cream would melt,* they ate it first, before their sandwiches, with an air of surreptitious, surprised glee. The silver bowl was so cold that when my daughter's fingers touched the stem she left a print in the condensation and I felt it on my own fingers; the cold, and then the cold ice cream on her tongue, and the slight grittiness of the ice. My friend and I looked at each other with raised eyebrows and rolled our eyes: Where do they get this stuff? the look asked. The silver domes, the white bread with the crust cut off, the toothpicks, the Nesselrode pie, even the waiter? We drank the iced tea we had ordered, which came in tall glasses with lots of ice, and straws from which the bottom half of the paper had been torn, but not the top, so it was guaranteed that no hand had touched the part of the straw from which you were about to drink, and I thought of the months, long ago, I had worked for an old man and how he liked his straws that way, with his lunch. Since he was a man who operated out of a deep sense of embarrassment and deference to others, I wondered briefly how he had made that desire—that *necessity* to him, that no one touch the straw—clear. The girls immediately blew hard through their straws, with snorting noises, so that the little bits of paper flew off and landed across the room, on the cool green tiles, and we reprimanded them, idly.

After a bit I had some errands to do across town, and I did them, and then I returned to the club in the terrible heat. The girls had had a wonderful time, swimming. By then my friend had left, and the girls were with a babysitter, a Russian woman who didn't speak English, so we bowed to each other in the lobby, and my daughter and I walked up York Avenue, in search of a taxi. There were none. It was so hot that you could see the city air in furred bands, rising from the buses. For a while it seemed that it would not be possible to get home at all: no buses came, and because it was 5 p.m., all the taxis, the way they do inexplicably, in New York, at the busiest times, had gone off duty. I found myself thinking, wildly, for a moment, that we could not get home because we were *stuck in time*—there was no way to get from the cool glade of that pool, and the waiter and the silver domes, and the toothpicks, to the next place we were meant to be, meeting her brother at a pizza place, in West Harlem, where we live. The force field of the past was strong, a whirlpool—it was inexplicable to me that I was the mother of the girl, in a damp sundress, and not the girl herself, forty years earlier, eating an identical sandwich under a silver dome, at a different club, with my cousin's grandmother, who wore stockings in the summer, before we would have to wait for thirty minutes to get into the pool.

We crossed the smoky street and I bought two bottles of water from a Mexican vendor, on the corner of Sixty-first. We drank them down. I tried to remind myself that my daughter and I would certainly reach home. That it was only three miles, if we needed to walk, when we got there we could order in, if we liked, and turn on the air conditioner in the bedroom, and take a cool shower. That this was infinitely better than the plight of other women and children around the globe, or even, I knew, in the city in which we lived, and I should stop feeling sorry for myself. It worked, a little, but not enough. I wanted, still, to be the girl in the Speedo tank suit who was told I had to wait thirty minutes before getting into the water.

The west side of the street was a little cooler. Up its artery swam a taxi whose light blinked on. My daughter ran toward it and flagged it down. It was full of priests. Smiling and nodding they got out, and the last one, a Russian Orthodox priest dressed in full black regalia in the heat, held the door open, and we sped uptown, to meet her brother at a restaurant that had sprung up two blocks from our house, an address from which only a few years ago there had been not one restaurant in a radius of eight blocks, which is a continent in the city. It was called, inexplicably, the Bad Horse. The children liked it because the pizza was good, and it was cool, and I liked it because they turn the music down if you can make yourself heard to ask.

The Bad Horse had not been there, three weeks ago. A young couple, my neighbor had told me, was trying to make a go of it. I tried to remember what had been there before, and hoped it had not been another restaurant, which would mean that the neighborhood, waking itself from its slumber, had already developed its own impossibilities, its particular Bermuda Triangles where nothing could flourish but FOR RENT signs.

Why was the horse bad? The waiters didn't know. But the name made me think of another new restaurant, on the site of an old one. This one, the old one, was a restaurant I had been to a hundred times, over the years. I had begun coming to it in the butterflied chicken phase when we were feeling flush, and momentarily poised to enter another life, in which we could regularly afford the mediocre food and the good drink it provided, under its once risqué murals of woodland nymphs. Later, I went to drink pear champagne at the bar, with a man I would marry, who, my father said, was the only man he ever knew who didn't look like a gangster in a double-breasted suit—he was too fey, too elegant—and when we moved from the bar we would sit at table thirty-eight, where we had decided to get married, catty-corner to the mirrors. Later, we took the children, and they ate pasta with butter and later, roast chicken. The restaurant was in the lobby of the apartment building where the poet Robert Lowell had died, in a taxi, outside the front door, returning to his second wife after a hiatus, so there was that, too. In a room across the lobby, which also belonged to the restaurant, was the "Little Bar," you could still smoke, and sit at small tables where your knees knocked into the knees of whomever you were with, which was the point, anyway. The last time I was there it was to meet a friend, a playwright, who was dying, and whose nurse took her to the door and then she made her way to the table where I was waiting, with a walker, and when she sat down said, *Thank God for drink.*

A while ago, after the ballet, we would go and sit at the bar. The bartender's name was Victor, and he would put a stand of boiled eggs in front of me, because he knew I liked them, and we drank champagne. There was a man who almost always sat at the very end of the bar, whom my husband didn't like—he felt he had been criminal, about some deal, that I never quite understood—so we avoided his glance in the mirror, and he usually left before we did. Victor had a son at the Naval Academy, in Annapolis. Sometimes, but not often, we had a little something to eat; often even if we didn't order, Victor would give us something, anyway, a bit of smoked salmon, or a piece of cake. At that time I had a fur coat, that a friend had given me and I had had made over, with a blue silk lining, and I held it on my lap rather than check it. Sometimes in the winter I draped it over my shoulders. Victor always asked my husband what I would have. What he said was, "And for Mrs. Joe?"

When he said it I felt that all was right with the world, the world I had made, or tried to make. I liked having the warm, light coat and the glass of champagne, or sometimes Sancerre, and the little plate of something to eat, and the man my husband didn't like at the end of the bar. I knew, I felt, how to be that person. That that person was someone invented out of another time, and if her constellate points had vanished it didn't concern me, then, nor that the wavery mirror in the leaf-green powder room where I sometimes went to check my reflection showed me the girl in the Speedo suit, waiting to get into the water. About the time we decided we couldn't afford to go to the ballet every week during the season, nor could we afford other things, the restaurant closed. The owner, a Hungarian, had died, too, and it was sold.

To me at the time the restaurant closing seemed to be of a piece, another square filled in the ghost grid. When I spoke to my friend who lives in the country, I told him about it, and he said, "Well, another thing we won't ever do again." The other night I was walking past Sixty-seventh Street with another old friend, with whom I had never been to the restaurant, although we had each been there many times, with other people. Let's look, I said. I had heard it had recently been reopened, in the same spot. You could no longer go into the restaurant through the lobby of the apartment building; this had been regularized. There was a door marked THE LEOPARD. We went in, hesitant. Some of the murals had been kept, and the odd way you had to climb a small step to get to the back where the bar was. But the bar was on the other side of the restaurant, the wrong side, sleek, an expanse of shining wood. Victor wasn't there. The girl in the Speedo suit put her toe in the water, and withdrew it.

Mr. Ferri and the Furrier

When I saw, in the newspaper, that Mr. Ferri had died I immediately thought of the furrier. It may have been the association of consonants or vowels—I almost wrote "consolation," and "constellation" would be most accurate—of a hands-on caress, a kind of attention to detail and to the customer that barely exists anymore, like cigarette lighters, or loose powder, or the still click of a phone being lifted up, somewhere else in the house, when you are speaking on it, too softly, in another room. Mr. Ferri, who as far as I know was no relation to the great ballerina Alessandra Ferri, though he shared some of the dancer's wit and grace, her deft movements, although his were often close to the ground, and he danced, always, as a partner rather than a soloist—a wren of a man with pins flashing in his teeth. Mr. Ferri was a tailor. His shop was four flights above Madison Avenue, in the East Sixties. On the street level was a fashionable restaurant, and across the street was and is a line of some of the most expensive jewelers in the world: in one, a bird of paradise made entirely of diamonds, the size of the flower; in another, a sapphire large as a robin's egg. But the door to Mr. Ferri's was sandwiched between the restaurant and a dress shop that catered to fairies of the woodland, the dresses all tulle and peau de soie; some of which, secretly, would make their way to Mr. Ferri's agency a half hour, or a decade, after they left the shop.

I had first heard of Mr. Ferri from my friend Sara. We were on the beach in late August, talking idly of things we planned to do in the fall. Sara needed a new rug. I had a jacket—I think it was a jacket—I needed altered, and Sara directed me to Mr. Ferri. When Sara and I were young we worked in the office of a magazine, and in those days—it was the early 1980s—she dressed out of a bandbox. Her shoes matched her dress, and she had the sheeny beauty of the girls who advertised Breck shampoo. One afternoon many years after this—it was fall, and the red leaves of the turning maples were flush against the window of the house where we were sitting together, because it was raining—we made a list of those outfits. There was a white pleated wool skirt with a matching sweater appliquéd with a blue and red anchor; a pink sleeveless dress with what used to be called a jewel neckline and for all I know still is; a navy-blue linen shirtwaist with a rope belt. Over time these outfits were shed for loose blue jeans and men's shirts, never ironed. Instead of a Breck girl she now looks like a gelatin print of Georgia O'Keeffe. It did not occur to me that she would know of a tailor, then, on the Upper East Side. But she did know of Mr. Ferri, as I knew of a rug dealer, to whom she subsequently went, although I do not know if she bought a rug from him, because by that time she had also bought a house, and was then in that state in which it is difficult to buy just one thing.

I am trying now to remember my first visit to Mr. Ferri. I had a shopping bag over my arm, and I had stopped first at one of the jewelry stores across the street, the shop on the corner whose door and portico were made of bronze: I had once written a story about a pair of emerald earrings at that shop which had been stolen from a pirate ship, and since then my girls and I had made it a regular stop on our walks up and down the East Side, from their school, to visit their great-great-aunt, who was immobilized by a stroke in her apartment, which smelled of beeswax and Norell, next to the Guggenheim Museum, or to buy school shoes, at a place called Ricky's, where my mother had bought shoes for me as a child. The staff at the jewelry store, which was owned by a man who had started his career by selling Mexican wedding dresses in the East Village, was genial about letting them try on tiaras and necklaces that had belonged to queens and grand dames, and I had made a friend of a girl who worked there, who wore her cap of black hair in a helmet, like a Valkyrie. "What's in the bag?" she asked.

It was a disreputable-looking large plastic bag, with the kind of hard plastic handles that click together if you line them up properly, which is hard to do, and it was printed in red and blue letters with the name of a local drugstore chain. In the hushed space of the shop it was outré, a nanny goat in the Tuileries. I pulled out the contents to show her.

The first thing was the jacket I had been thinking about on the beach. It was a heavy wool houndstooth hacking jacket. The teeth were brown, moss green, and gold, and the top of the collar was lined with wool flannel like cat fur. I was then under the impression that the jacket had belonged to my immobilized aunt. She had given it to me two decades ago. Since then I had replaced the buttons. When I held it up we could both see that the pale lining was torn to shreds. The other item in the bag was a pair of dark brown velvet trousers. The velvet was made of silk, and it had been rubbed almost away in some places. Those places, on the knees, looked mottled. I had bought the trousers almost twenty years ago. They had a high, fitted waistband and bell-bottoms. I had been happy in them. I had worn them with a white poet's blouse and flat shoes, and in the winter, when I went out, with a black velvet hooded parka with a drawstring waist. The worst of the wear was on the seat, which had split, which I had tried to fix, but had torn again. The Valkyrie looked at the jacket and the trousers. She reached out a hand and felt the velvet. "Well," she said, "waste not, want not."

The last thing in the bag was wrapped in white tissue paper. I drew it out and unwrapped it. I had not meant to show it to her out of a kind of shyness; the jacket and trousers had come a little close to airing dilapidation, or even dirty laundry. But maybe because of that, I wanted to create a frisson of surprise to detract from my feeling of haplessness. Inside were the two yards of silk I was bringing to Mr. Ferri, to replace the jacket's shredded lining. I had called to make an appointment. The man who answered the telephone had repeated the number when he answered. He sounded as if he had a mouthful of pins. I thought, unbidden, of the tailor of Gloucester, with his fine silver whiskers, a story which I had read aloud to my children countless times, and which had always terrified me. A tailor sends his cat, Simpkin, out to buy a twist of cherry-colored wool. The mayor is getting married the next morning, and the sumptuous waistcoat he has ordered is unfinished. We know, though Beatrix Potter does not tell us, that the tailor is disorganized, untidy, prone to fits and starts. Before the cat leaves (we understand, too, that the tailor can talk to the cat, and that he is the only helper the tailor can afford), the cat imprisons his enemies, a family of mice, under a set of teacups. The mice scrabble under the teacups. The tailor discovers the captives, releases them, and angers the cat, who hides the twist. The tailor falls ill, in despair, realizes he cannot finish the waistcoat, but grateful mice creep out at night and embroider the waistcoat so magnificently that the enfeebled tailor is overwhelmed when he arrives at the shop the next morning, wringing his hands. The shop is empty. One button is left undone. A note next to the buttonhole, written in tiny script, reads "No more twist." The cat, cajoled, recovers his good humor, and supplies the bit of cherry thread. It is based on a true story. The rattling of teacups, filled with fur and tails, the malignant cat, the sheer improbability of it coming right.

"Nelson Ferri, YUkon 8-5850" said the voice, full of pins and needles. I came to. The mouse headed out for the territories. My grandmother's telephone number was CHelsea-3. My great-aunt's was ATwater-9, another aunt's, TRafalgar-7. These numbers, all of them abandoned, made a ticker tape in my mind. I could not remember my first New York telephone number. The exchange at the magazine where Sara and I had worked, to which she wore her matching shoes and bag, was ALgonquin-4. These numbers, all of them abandoned, were colored places on a folded map. On the telephone, speaking to the voice of the man holding pins in his mouth, I explained I needed the lining of a jacket replaced, that he had been recommended by my friend. Length? Size? "Two yards," he said.

In the jewelry store I unwrapped the fabric. I had bought it the week before, in the pouring rain, in the garment district, from a shop I had visited obsessively years before. It was during a period in my life when the amount of time that I devoted to thinking about upholstery fabric was in inverse proportion to everything else I wasn't thinking about: chief among these was how a person like me, untrained in domestic arts or stick-to-itiveness, could be responsible for a baby, who would quickly grow up into a child. I slipcovered one hand-me-down sofa in ill-advised pale duck linen, with striped piping. By the second year I had dyed it with tea, to hide the stains. But by the time I found myself propelled to Mr. Ferri I had long given up on slipcovers and upholstery—draping the multiplying chairs and sofas with old tablecloths and shawls, as one child, by hook or crook, had followed another, and many of my sentences, then, were prefaced by the words "there's just no point in . . ." I had not looked at the fabric since I bought it—the shop had wrapped it, like a present, in carefully folded tissue paper. It slid across the glass counter, like a half-vanished dream.

The silk was printed with figures. The colors were red and gray and slate blue and moss green—I see now the colors on my telephone map, the same sepia palette—as if the fabric had overlaid or colored in that paint-by-numbers graph of the city. The figures were between four and six inches high: they were Japanese people, in nineteenth-century dress, fingering abaci, mending shoes, surveying their own collections of silk. The signal note was quiet industry. There were no conversations: each figure was intent on its own business. The men wore blue or red pantaloons, and pigtails. Their hats were tied underneath their chins with ribbons. When I was a child my grandparents came back from a trip and gave me a book of lavishly illustrated Japanese folktales, by Lafcadio Hearn. There was a story about a talking fish, and another about the fountain of youth, which held no interest for me, and one in which a dragon shed ruby tears. It was called "The Boy Who Drew Cats," and it was the title story which frightened me: a boy loves to draw cats; he is the youngest child of a large family, and instead of doing his chores, he draws cats leaping, sleeping, eating, dreaming. In despair, his parents take him to the village monastery in hopes that he might become a priest. But still, he draws cats. The abbot, too, despairs of him, and sends him off, advising him to avoid large places at night, and favor small ones. He wanders, despondent, and then sees a large temple, where a light is burning. The temple is deserted. He does not know it, but a huge goblin-rat has scared the priests away, and the warriors who have been sent to capture the goblin have all vanished. All that remains in the temple are some large screens, covered with white rice paper. Unable to resist, he takes out his pen and draws cats on the rice paper walls: the most beautiful cats he has ever drawn, and then, recalling the priest's advice, he climbs into a tiny cupboard, and falls asleep. He is woken in the night by the sound of a terrible battle: hissing and sharp cries, but when he wakes in the morning the temple is quiet and full of light. In the center of the room is the gigantic goblin-rat, dead, and the cats he has drawn on the screen have blood on their mouths. *Twist, twist.*

I recognized the pantaloons from the illustration in the story: they were the costume worn by the priest in the temple, who sends the little boy who drew cats to slay the goblin. "Goodness," said the Valkyrie, about the silk lining, and ran her hand over the silent faces. A customer had come in; one who was more likely than I ever would be to buy a pair of drop rosette earrings, which I had tried on a few weeks earlier, and admired. I was late. I folded up the fabric and put it in the plastic bag with the trousers and the jacket, and went out the door and across the street, to find Mr. Ferri.

Later, when I brought my daughter there, with a jade silk dress over her arm that needed to be altered, she said, "Are you *sure?*" We disregarded the tiny elevator, which I knew was at the end of the hall, and instead climbed the three flights of listing steps, which were covered in cracked linoleum. But the first time I went I wasn't sure. The distance from the jewelry shop and the Valkyrie, and even the flower stand and the fashionable restaurant, called, I think, Fred's or Jacques's, was too abrupt. The shabby hall and the zigzag staircase were a split seam. That Mr. Ferri's business was to turn a sow's ear into a silk purse, and that the look of the place where that happened didn't matter, hovering as it did between the seen and the unseen, in proximity to possibility, I didn't know yet, or understand. At the pasteboard door I rang the bell. When no one answered I turned the knob. The door opened to a rectangular room divided, at one end, by a counter, and behind the counter were some cutting tables, covered with rolls of fabric and measuring tapes. At the other end was what looked like a dressing room, with a curtain across it on a wooden pole. The gray carpet was so littered with pins it glittered. The room was dominated by a tall open three-sided mirror. In front of it was a low wooden stool. Two men with black hair shiny with brilliantine, in their late twenties or early thirties, were working behind the counter. A small elderly gray man, his shirt stuck here and there with pins, his eyes magnified behind his glasses, was Mr. Ferri. I had made an appointment, and he greeted me by name. "You have the jacket with you?" he asked.

I nodded. I took the jacket out of the bag. I had not repacked the lining fabric as neatly as I'd hoped. A foot or two came out with it, a fan of faces, so I piled it on the counter as well, with the jacket, which Mr. Ferri immediately took up in his hands. "Johnny, can I have a hanger, please?"

A hanger appeared. It was an old heavy wooden hanger with a worn peeling label, black with gold letters, which read THE NEW YORKER HOTEL. Mr. Ferri hung the jacket on the hanger, on a hook. Then he began to touch the fabric and turn it over in his hands, looking at the sleeves and then the shoulders. He touched the buttons, and then turned back the lapels. Once I had seen a man look over a horse he was thinking of buying, and Mr. Ferri and the way he appraised the jacket reminded me of that day, the sun and shadow and smell of hay. It was hot in the room. I was wearing a black cardigan sweater and I took it off. Mr. Ferri gave me a long look, considering. "Could you turn around, please?" I did. Again, I thought of my friend and the horse. He took the jacket off the hanger and handed it to me. "Could you put it on, please?"

I had not worn it for some time and it smelled faintly of cedar and old dry cleaning fluid. He walked around me, and then took some pins out of his mouth and hovered for a moment behind me. I felt the weight of the jacket shift. "If we take it in here, then it will hang better, so. And when the lining is replaced the jacket will hang better, too, because it will know what's what."

What's what. "What's what," I would learn on my visits to

Mr. Ferri, was a magical term. It meant that a garment was finished, and it also referred to that state of precise rightness to which every dress, jacket, or pair of trousers aspired: to be itself, but more so, to be, as far as he could make it so, perfect. Before I took the jacket off he considered shortening the sleeve one-quarter inch, then rejected the idea, and in doing so touched the inside of my wrist, briefly, with his thumb, as if taking my pulse. *No, fine, fine.* The moment was gone. When I took out the lining I had brought he did not blink. He unrolled it on the countertop, then said that as there was not enough for the sleeves, could they (he said "we") use another lining instead? He showed me a bolt of silk the color of milky tea. We agreed. The lining of the sleeves would not show, in any case.

"And you will have your nice secret anyway," he said, his finger passing over the faces of the silent marketplace.

The torn trousers were the work of a moment. He would try to replace the place that had been rent and worn through by taking a patch from the inside of the pant leg hem; he wasn't sure it would hold. Did I want to try anyway? The material was beautiful but like many beautiful things it wore easily. About this he spoke less like a Prospero and more like a physician: Was the patient worth saving? We agreed on life support.

"Now we will get busy, busy, and you will come back next week." Sara had warned me that the custom was to pay half the bill, in cash, up front. I had just enough for the bill which Mr. Ferri's Johnny wrote up and presented to me without a word.

It was October, and it got colder. I picked up my jacket with its iridescent panels of silent faces, and the trousers, which I would wear twice before they split again. I walked through Central Park with the large plastic bag that Mr. Ferri had carefully folded and saved for me. I did not know, that day, that as I walked through the park, which seemed to turn from Indian summer to autumn in an afternoon, the house that I was walking toward was slowly splitting apart, nor that I would wear the jacket almost constantly through the next several winters, the secret lining close to my skin. I had recently heard from an old friend, to whom I had written when his father died, and whom I had not spoken to since we were young. We had lived together in New York and often walked through the park together, and I found myself on that afternoon missing him: he had grown up with his friends in the park, and because of that the park to me was part of not only our history together but his dream-life, which had become mine, when we lived together and for long afterward. The fall was the beginning of a gyroscope, in which I would come out the other end and there would be another voice, not my friend's, but someone else's whose I had known even longer, whom when I told him that I had walked across the park would immediately ask what shoes I was wearing, because he is trying to dissuade me from the fashionable shoes he loves—his great-grandfather was a shoemaker in Italy, and I think he longs to have been one—which I persist in wearing, and which tear at my feet.

But then I had no inkling of this. It got colder, and because the teetering house was so expensive to heat, I was sitting in a room at the front of the house one evening wrapped in a blanket, looking out at the street, which was covered with snow, and pretending to write a letter, when the telephone rang. It

was my friend E——. Her husband had decided he would like
to buy her a new fur coat, and would I like her old one? The
coat, a mink, was twenty years old. She had thought of using
it to line a raincoat, but she already had a fur-lined raincoat
which was perfectly functional. She didn't need another. It was
old, but it was warm—the mink, that is. The wool blanket
I was wrapped in was black-and-red plaid. It had belonged
to my first husband's grandmother, and the moths had long
ago webbed the corners. For a while, it had covered one of the
tattered sofas in the living room, but when it became tattered
itself, I had taken it upstairs. As I talked on the phone, I stuck
my finger through the holes the moths had made.

Later that week I picked up the coat from her doorman.
Like many buildings in New York, it was a building I had
known a long time ago. Almost every day when she was small
I had picked up my youngest daughter at her school and rid-
den through the green river of Central Park. The bus stopped
in front of the awning of this same building, where we got off,
before turning right and then left, to the subway, which would
take us farther uptown. When I was a girl, a friend of mine
knew a girl who lived there, whose mother, she told me, was
clairvoyant. No matter what her friend was doing, or where
she was, her mother would later describe places she herself
had never seen. When the girl went to college, her mother
would call, and tell her what she was wearing. The story—
the mother, peering through the ether at the other end of the
phone—haunted me. The girl always had plenty of pocket
money, but one of the things she liked to do was hail a cab
that was about to go through the park at Eighty-first, and get
the driver to take her across the park for free, since, she rea-

soned, he was going anyway. Part of this story was always that she told the cabbie she "didn't have a nickel." What difference a nickel would have made was unclear, but the point was the old-fashioned diction, the plaintive quality—she was a small, fine-boned girl, with hair the color of toffee, who looked a little like a mouse. Often she would succeed—my friend had been with her on more than one mission—and implicit, too, was the sense of danger, of getting away with something for nothing, of lying, and also, the neatness of the solution: Why not? The upshot of this is that when I went to see my friend and her husband at their immaculate apartment, with walls made of planed timber from exotic trees, and when I got off the bus with my daughter after school, and when I tried to get a cab on that corner, I was at once there, at no. 7, and also the girl looking through the wrong end of a telescope, all those years ago, a fortune-teller, who could see me, who had become, too, a woman at the end of the phone being offered a fur coat, or squinting, wrapped in an ancient red-and-black blanket, listening to her own children on the phone, who were away at school, and trying to picture where they were calling from.

I picked up the coat and went around the corner to take the subway home. At home, I left it in the hall and went to make supper. It wasn't until later that evening that I remembered the coat. I brought the bag upstairs and tried it on. It felt hot, heavy, and stiff. I thought of the rule about fires that had never made intuitive sense to me: if someone is burning, wrap them up in a carpet. It was hot inside the coat. In the inadequate bedroom mirror, all I could see was my face peering out of a cloud of fur. I went upstairs to the third floor, to ask the children. Two of them were sitting on the long red sofa by the top landing, with what looked like a set of math problems on the floor, abandoned, beside them. When they saw me, in the coat, they immediately began to snort with laughter. *What is that?* they demanded. The general opinion was that it looked like I had had a fight with a bear and it had won. I looked, my daughter said, like a gigantic black cat. I pointed out that it wasn't bear or cat, it was mink. They asked whether I really intended to wear fur. When I replied that in all likelihood the mink had been dead many many years and whether I wore it or not it was not going to bring it back to life, the response was gagging noises and sobs, and then the sound of a tom-tom made by hitting an old leather chair cushion with a stick, and I decided to leave them to it.

I went back downstairs and looked at the fur in the mirror. *What's what?* I thought. The coat was too big. There was a tear in the left sleeve and a hole in the pocket. A button was missing. *Twist, twist.* When I was in high school I'd found a lipstick in the pocket of an old coat of my father's, and when I unscrewed it the dried red lipstick broke in my hand. There was nothing in the pockets of the coat. I had never imagined myself as the owner of a fur coat, and I was having trouble imagining it now. A friend of many years had an aunt who had owned a dress business on Madison Avenue in the sixties and seventies: Perhaps she would know what to do with the coat? I had called on her before, my friend's Aunt Susan: she had led me to the shop where I'd found the Japanese silk lining. The advice was definite. There was a furrier called Jerry Sorbara, and I was to take the coat to him. She didn't have his address, but as far as she could recall he was in the East Thirties. Out

of loyalty, I called Mr. Ferri. He was regretful but firm: no fur.
I had an evening dress of my mother's I was thinking of having him look at—we arranged a time that week. Then I called
Jerry Sorbara. The woman who answered the telephone had a
high nasal voice: she sounded like the telephone operator at
the switchboard at the magazine where Sara and I had worked
so long ago, a Gorgon matched by her Medusa of wires. She
asked me how old the fur was, which she called "your mink."
I told her. Then added, out of nervousness—here was a new
gamut to run. "Approximately, I mean, I think." There was a
long silence. Then she said, "Anytime."

It was not a neighborhood I knew well. On the way downtown I had had lunch with a friend, in a restaurant behind
the Fifth Avenue Public Library, which looks out on Bryant
Park and the pigeons scuffling in the fall leaves. She started
when her foot knocked into the bag under the table, which I
had refused to check. The fur felt electric and alive, and she
said, "What *is* that?" I had walked the ten blocks south on
Fifth Avenue, past the Public Library and the old B. Altman.
When I found the address, between a Korean grocer and a
restaurant advertising fried pork and kimchi, the porter at the
desk waved me in: I wanted, he said, the eleventh floor. There
was a long mirror in the lobby and in it, I saw an arm of the
coat hanging outside the bag, like the arm of a beaver or a
badger. It gave me a feeling of distress. In the mirror I looked
blanched and uneasy, fish-eyed.

It was the kind of elevator my youngest child once called
two-faced. The door that opened onto the eleventh floor was
not the door which had opened in the lobby: it was another,
secret door, and it opened behind me. I walked into a small

white cubicle, where a woman was seated behind a glass partition. There were pieces of fur on hooks on the wall behind her, and it was hard not to think she was stuffed. I said my name. "You have your mink?"

Immediately I wanted to say that it wasn't my mink, it was my friend's mink: the idea of having a mink, which seemed to me, in that moment, indescribably vulgar, was something I wanted to put away from me, especially a mink that was lying scrunched in a shopping bag, its one badger arm testing the air. There was no help for it. "Jimmy," she yelled, and pressed a button. A door to the left was opened by a very tall man, about ten or fifteen years younger than I was. He was wearing a pin-striped suit, and his black hair was cut short, and parted on the side. He had the handsome face of a television sports announcer, and I took the coat out of the bag and on his instruction, put it on. As I look back now that this was a time of my life when I was constantly trying things on, in workrooms and dressing rooms, and asking people what they thought, which is not something I do often now, for complex and perplexing reasons—why I was doing that and why I ceased to do it. Jimmy looked like a man on television who is trying to make the best of what he knows is going to be a sad, losing game. "Aha!" he said, rubbing his hands. And then, "Aha!" again, as if in the interval he had come to some kind of conclusion. A discussion ensued. I asked if it was possible to alter the coat. I think the expression I used was "Is it worth it?" When I entered the room, a spacious atelier with three standing mirrors, and coats grouped on hangers on trees, as well as along the wall, Jimmy had just finished helping three clients, a mother and her two daughters. They were buying a coat each.

They were so harsh with each other that it was impossible not to think of Cinderella's stepmother and evil sisters. When one tried on a coat that didn't suit her—the color was wrong, or the style—the others were beside themselves with glee, pointing out the flaws, and how it would be impossible, actually, for Sylvia to wear *anything like that.* It seemed impossible that they had found coats that they did like, although they had, apparently, as each one walked out with a box under her arm, after a consultation about whether it would be possible to ship the coats to Boca Raton, and therefore evade paying taxes. I did not think that the expression "is it worth it?" had occurred to Sylvia and her mother and sister, and I felt embarrassed. What was I doing there?

I realized in that moment that I wanted a fur coat. It had not occurred to me to want one before. I looked at Jimmy with a kind of pleading. The fur was old, he told me. The quality was good, but it could tear if they tried to cut it up. I should try some coats on—what style was I thinking of? For the next few minutes I tried on furs. In all of them, I looked ridiculous. My children were right. I looked like a woman being eaten by an animal. Or Ninotchka. Jimmy and I were as one on this. Fifteen minutes later, I had tried on ten coats. A short man who looked like a wrestler, called Greg, who would a year or two later sell me, as a sample, a leftover fox hat from the previous season, for what used to be called a song, was taking up the discarded coats and tenderly hanging them up again, but still there was a mounting pile of fur on the leather sofa. "My mink" was on the table. The last coat I tried on was a short car coat, with a cable belt. Behind my image in the mirror a man appeared. He was small, and wore a golf shirt, pressed trousers, a snakeskin belt, and white tennis shoes. His hair was white. He had a small cleft chin and molded cheekbones, and he looked like a small elderly version of Robert Mitchum in *The Sundowners.* He came up behind me, shook his head, and lifted the jacket off my shoulders. He said, under his breath, "No, no, no," and then, aloud, "What is going on here?"

Jimmy explained that this was his father. I had brought in an old fur, and wanted a new coat. I protested. He explained I wanted a new coat made of my old coat. The older man walked over to the table and looked at my mink, and then at me. He disappeared, and came back a moment later, with a coat over his arm. He held the coat open for me to step into, then stepped back. "There. Here is your coat."

The coat was cut small in the shoulders, and tapered out from a fitted bodice to a slight bell that stopped at the knees. The sleeves were narrow. The coat had a spread collar that could be worn up or down, against the cold. A line of three buttons stopped just above the waist. It reminded me of a coat I had loved as a child, what my mother called a party coat, which had been passed down to me by a cousin. It was made of pale blue tweed, and it had a dark blue velvet collar. This was that coat, grown up. Was it possible to buy this coat? I asked. It was. Jimmy looked it up. It cost four times, almost exactly, more than I had ever paid for a car. I shook my head. I explained that this wasn't possible. I had four children, all of whom had to be fed, and who attended school. There was no place in my life for this coat. The older man, who by now I had learned was Jerry, the Jerry of Jerry Sorbara, Jimmy's father, went back over to the table and picked up "my mink." He turned it around in his hands as if it were a living animal, and

I thought again of Mr. Ferri, and my friend I had watched buy a horse. The horse had stood still in the barn, his black coat coal in the sun and shadow, smelling of salt and sweat. The mink smelled faintly of Cabouchard. Then he put it down. He looked at Greg. "Get me the pattern for the Audrey," he said.

"*What?*" said Jimmy.

Greg left the room and returned with an accordion fan made out of onionskin paper. When I was a child my mother sewed some of her own clothes and clothes for my sister and me from Butterick and Vogue patterns. She had an old-fashioned Singer sewing machine. The machine had been given to her by her parents, my grandparents, for her sixteenth birthday, and part of the story was that the machine was "top of the line." My grandfather had decided to buy his daughter a machine, but it wasn't going to be "any old machine." Another part of the story was that they made payments each month for a year, of sixteen dollars each: the real point of the the story was that when my mother was growing up, her parents didn't have enough money to buy the "top of the line machine" "upfront." That this was the same as buying on credit didn't occur to me.

My mother always told this story with a kind of pleasure, her parents loved her enough to buy her the sewing machine, to buy the machine was a sacrifice, they had to "put money aside," and inside the story was a complicated kernel, inside an apricot pit: it was a virtue to be poor, to not have enough, to know "what's what." And then the machine itself, given to a girl one generation away from the Triangle Shirtwaist Factory fire, who liked to sew. When my daughter told me this story again, the other night, as it had been told to her by her grandmother, once again, recently, she said, expostulating, "Why did they buy it if they couldn't afford it? Why did they tell her that?"

An argument, biting its tail. The patterns my mother used, in the sewing room under the eaves in the house I grew up in. The house was shaded by tulip trees that shed their long yellowing petals into the ivy beds. The patterns were made of onionskin paper, the color of those flowers. In the summer I found the carapaces of beetles, stiff, amber. The onionskin paper, I knew, was not made of real onion skin. My mother pinned the cloth to the ghostly pattern with straight pins and then cut the cloth. She also knew how to cut out paper dolls, and showed me.

Greg lay the paper pattern carefully on the hardwood floor. Mr. Sorbara pulled a tape measure from his sleeve. As Greg read out the measurements he ran the tape lightly along my arms, across my back and shoulders, and from my neck to the back of my knee. He asked me to hold the tape when he measured the circumference of my hips. The sleeves would be lengthened, he said, one quarter of an inch. "Like this," he said, and held his forefinger and thumb together, and laid them, as Mr. Ferri had, on my wrist. Perched on the table on the side of the room, Jimmy's face contorted. *"Pop,"* he said.

Mr. Sorbara looked at me. "First we will send out your mink, and we will bring it back to life. Then you will come back in two weeks, and we will try on the coat we will make for you."

"Dad," said Jimmy.

Mr. Sorbara ignored him. I said, "I think we have to talk

about what this is going to cost." I was a person who had been treated with kindness who had offered in return the carcass of a cat.

He asked me what I could spend. I told him.

Jimmy asked his father if he could speak to him, privately. They left the room. From behind the closed door I could hear Jimmy's raised voice, and an answering, softer murmur. Mr. Sorbara came back into the room by himself. He smiled. He said, "We will see you in two weeks."

In the end, it was almost two months before my coat was finished. In the interim I made three trips to the showroom. Each time I looked for the door between the kimchi stands, half expecting it to have disappeared, and rode up to the eleventh floor in the Janus elevator. The same woman sat behind the glass partition, and each time I was ushered in by Jimmy, who rolled his eyes when he saw me, and buzzed for his father, who then soundlessly appeared. Once he was wearing carpet slippers. The first time he was apologetic; they had thought the coat would be ready. I was given to understand that my mink, which was now called "the coat," was a special case. The second time the coat, basted together, was taken in at the shoulders. "Stand up straight, my darling," said Mr. Sorbara. He put a finger to my third vertebra and pressed. "Here." When I raised my chin I heard my spine crack.

The day I went to pick up my coat there was a thin layer of ice on the ground. Steam rose from the vents outside the kimchi shop. In the showroom there was frost on the window. Greg brought the coat out in a garment bag. Did I want to try it on? I did. The fur gleamed. The coat stopped short of the knee, and closed with three horn buttons. Inside, on the lining

I had dropped off one afternoon, bought from the same shop where the year before I had found my Japanese merchants, my initials, the initials I had then, were embroidered in lilac thread. The lining was watered silk, pale blue and lavender, printed in marbleized swirls that reminded me of handmade endpapers I had first seen on a trip to Florence, on wooden racks, when I did not have enough money to buy even a single sheet. The print was called "Florentine."

For once, Jimmy was in the room. He was rolling his eyes. "Do you have any idea . . . ?" he said to me.

Mr. Sorbara and I looked at my reflection in the pier glass. We saw a woman with her dark hair pulled up and back, in jeans and flat shoes, wearing a narrow dark mink coat that just grazed her knees. He put the collar up. "Very pretty," he said. In the mirror I gave him an inquiring look. He shrugged, then said, "You are a young woman. This coat looks very nice on you. This is your first fur coat, but it will not be your last."

In the mirror, Jimmy raised his eyes, appealing to heaven. Then he said, "Be careful of the lining. Fur we can fix, but if you tear that, we'll have to redo the whole thing."

The fur tore. They fixed it. I am careful when I take off the coat and put it on my lap, when I wear it to the movies, to fold it fur side out. I have not bought another fur coat. I did buy the black fox hat, one September, from Greg, when I picked up my coat from storage. I did not go to see Mr. Ferri for a number of years, and then I read that he had died. The last dress I brought to be tailored was a silk taffeta orange-and-blue plaid evening gown, which I had inherited. Mr. Ferri was ill. Someone else hovered over me, with pins in his mouth, but the project was not a success. It may have been the dress, or my idea of what I wanted the dress to be, or me, and nothing to do with Mr. Ferri's absence, his touch on my wrist, at all. But the years in which I went to see Mr. Ferri, and had brought my friend E——'s coat to the furrier, had been a time in which I was happy to make over what came my way, to make do with what was given to me, often almost by accident, the world opening its arms: jackets, dresses, houses, love. They could be fixed with scissors, glue, cherry twist, pins. In those days I mixed flour and water paste, and the children made collages out of what they found in the woods, and made elevators from cardboard boxes. I bought linings that without my knowing it reminded me of other stories, and I wore them close to the skin. It was a time when I knew what was what. I knew that the thing to do was to avoid large places after dark. When the children had bad dreams at night I put out my hand and asked them to give them to me. I thought that if I believed in what I could dream up the goblin-rat would fall dead. I did not believe that the world was a place where anything could happen. I thought then that it was possible to alter anything.

Two Pictures

When I was a small child I went on many Saturdays with my grandfather to the Museum of Modern Art. The museum was located where it is now, on Fifty-third Street, but then it was a different place. It was small, and intimate, and it was a place you went to look at pictures. In some ways the museum felt to me like an extension of my grandfather. My grandfather (he was my father's father) was a man of medium height, whose red hair had turned white by the time I knew him. He wore a small mustache. Though I know I saw him frequently in other seasons, I think of him wearing a gray overcoat and a black beret. He was a great reader, and a devotee of Spinoza, particularly. Later, when I was about twelve, and he was dying but did not know that yet, he told me that his favorite book was *The Magic Mountain,* and he gave it to me to read. His childhood, first in Russia and then in New York, where his stepfather was unkind to him, was repressive. He ran away, and then came back. He was a lawyer, but sometime in his middle years he became a painter. The room in which I stayed when I spent the weekend at my grandparents' apartment was his studio. It smelled of oil paint and turpentine.

On Saturday mornings after breakfast we took the E train to the museum. This was a convenient train, because the stop was directly outside my grandparents' building, in Chelsea, and it stopped on Fifty-third Street and Fifth Avenue. Often, in my memory, it was snowing. Because this was the early sixties, when little girls did not generally wear trousers, I wore heavy black serge tights, a smocked dress with a knitted cardigan, black patent-leather Mary Jane shoes, and a wool coat that pinched my neck when the top button was closed.

My grandfather was a member of the museum: he showed a little card and we were ushered in with a bit of ceremony by the guard. This was in the days when the museum was almost empty on a Saturday morning, and because of this, often our mornings there felt like private visits. My grandfather sometimes had a picture in mind that he wanted to look at. He was drawn, always, to the pictures by Braque and Cézanne, which were on the second floor. These were the paintings of his youth, and they excited him. He liked to look at pictures for a long time, and he showed me how to look, too. Sometimes he would take me, as on a journey, from one corner of the painting to another, explaining how the light and color were talking to each other. If he was feeling lighthearted he gave the blue, or the red, something to say, like "Hello" or "Do you think it will rain?" I was perhaps five or six at the time, and this never failed to amuse me.

When my grandfather was through looking, and we had passed through and said hello to a few friends, *The Starry Night* and Matisse's blue and green dancers, on the stairwell, which I loved with my whole heart, it was time for my paintings.

There were two. We visited each one, in turn, and as I had stood with my grandfather without tugging at him, or hopping on one foot, or saying that I was hungry, he stood and waited until I was finished looking. The first picture was *Guer-*

nica. Later I heard it said about *Guernica* that when you look at it you know all there is to know about war. No one, certainly not my grandfather, said anything like that to me, at the time. At some point I think he explained the circumstances of the picture to me, while we stood in front of it. Picasso had painted it after the German and Italian forces had bombed the town called Guernica during the Spanish Civil War. I knew Picasso from the other pictures he had painted that hung in the museum, of blue clowns and a girl with a flower.

This picture was not like those pictures. It was huge. The impression, looking at it, was that it was three dimensional: the painting was a room, and you were inside it. I remember it as the biggest painting in the museum but that may not be true. It looked so to me. It was hung on the third floor, between the elevators. It was then, at that time, the most violent image I had ever seen. I was not as a child allowed to watch much television; then, though, violent images were not usual fare for children, nor for anyone else. There was, as compared to now, a dearth of images.

My method for looking at the painting was the one I had learned from my grandfather. I looked at one corner at a time. Here in this corner was a woman screaming. Below her, a little to the left, a horse was screaming. What were they saying to each other? I couldn't answer. A woman's face came out of a cloud. A flowerpot lay in shards. I did not, and do not, even now, have the vocabulary. Perhaps there is none, for those screams.

Sometimes I stood at one end of the picture, and just looked, close up, at a little patch. From the little patch, it was hard to see what else was going on. On other visits I walked from one end of the canvas to the other, my head slightly averted, as if I weren't really looking. It was, I think, my first experience of voyeurism. Every time I returned to look at the painting I was surprised to find that it was painted in shades of black and white and gray. In my mind it was red. I was always careful not to look at the baby.

When I was done looking we went back through the galleries to see my other picture. Sometimes we had seen it already, because it was hung in a hall, on a separate, small wall, in the permanent gallery my grandfather liked to visit first. When this happened I simply took my turn looking, or sometimes I pretended not to see it, depending on my mood, and then we went back.

This picture was by Pavel Tchelitchew. It was called *Hide-and-Seek*. It was a painting of a green tree. The tree was green, and the sky around the tree was also green, and inside the tree, there were tiny faces of children. These children were trapped, and trying to get out. I could tell they wanted to get out by their faces. It was a nightmare tree. But if you knew to step back a little from the trunk of the tree, the arms and twigs of the tree were really capillaries, and the tree was inside the head of a girl. I think it was my grandfather who pointed this out to me. The girl was about my age. She had dreamed the tree, but the tree had taken root. What were the faces saying to each other? What was the girl saying to the tree? This picture so frightened me that when we were in the gallery and came upon it suddenly, I turned my back to it and looked down at my shiny shoes.

The other day—it is almost half a century later, and it is late afternoon—I was walking up from the beach, in late August. I was on the path set into the high dune, with my children and the children of my friend, and when we got to the top, the path and the parking lot were alive with huge dragonflies. The sky was a black whir. Because my children are older than the last time the dragonflies came around, when they were frightened of them (the dragonflies emerge on the dune every few years, as part of a mysterious cycle, like cicadas) one of them said, "Oh, they won't hurt you," and their little convoy passed under the hum to the car.

Most of the dragonflies were congregated on a path that runs to the right of the parking lot, if you are facing the beach. The path is smothered in June by beach roses, and in August, by rose hips. When I was a child there was a sign on that path, painted with a skull and crossbones. Under this sign a legend read NO ADMITTANCE. Across the path was a piece of chain. The road then led to an air force radar station. The station, its headlight sweeping the beach at night, kept watch for enemy missiles. One day, we knew, missiles would be launched toward us by the Soviet Union, but these would be stymied by radar. Now the sign is gone, and people climb up the path a little way in order to get cell phone reception.

I stood on the dune for a little while longer, watching and listening to the dragonflies. The last time they came they had almost driven me mad; I think now they were indicative of a frenzy I sensed but knew nothing about, inside myself, the way the endless wind, a few days before, the back side of the hurricane, seemed a slow slithering fuse on the sill, electric on my skin. But last month I was happy to see the dragonflies, if only because it meant that time had passed.

Behind me, a little girl came up the dune, following her mother. She was wearing a pink two-piece bathing suit that was falling down, and her head was huge on a neck that almost could not support it. She was dismayed by the dragonflies. Her mother, who had two older children, dragging towels and pails up the hill, took one look at her and said, "Oh, Annie, it's Dragonfly Alley."

That art can transform a whir of black wings, burnish it and give it back, is something we know, but what finds a home in the mind is a mystery. At the top of the dune the girl and her mother and I smiled at each other, at the edge of the parking lot: we knew all about wands, and wizards, and Diagon Alley. In Diagon Alley, does the wizard choose the wand, or does the wand choose the wizard? That my grandfather countenanced these visits to the two pictures, which I see now, from this distance, as morbid and obsessive, remains a mystery to me, but when I was a child it was with my grandfather that I felt safe.

Although both times I have been married it was to men to whom painting was important—one, like my grandfather, is a painter, and one is in the business of art—I know next to nothing about painting. Draw a house, my children say. My drawings look like hen scratches, my houses have lopsided windows. Smoke comes out of the crooked chimneys like pigs' tails. But that these two pictures no longer hang in the museum is something I find difficult to hold in my mind. *Guernica* was returned to Spain in 1997, although a life-size needlepoint replica hangs in the United Nations. *Hide-and-Seek* is out of fashion: when I called the museum I was told it was in storage. That neither of these pictures is there may be a reason that I don't like the new museum, which is cold and too big and has too many things to buy, like a department store. Both pictures were landscapes of terror. At the museum, I knew, you couldn't stand too close to the pictures, or touch them. I shifted from foot to foot, holding my grandfather's hand. *You are here,* the map said.

How can that be? I thought. But I knew it was true. The world was a glove, it could turn inside out. The pictures were about what I knew, and what I didn't know yet, but would. I knew that too. They were one way I learned about these things.

Going In

The beach we go to is the most beautiful beach in the world. This may sound like overstatement, but it is a statement of fact. It lies almost at the end of Cape Cod, where the hand of the Cape's flexed arm, extended into the Atlantic, turns and cups the bay. The bay is formed by the inner curve of that arm. In the summer, the house where we have stayed for many years—and where we may or may not remain, a niggling question that has just recently introduced itself, like the buzzing of a fly or the new, pernicious wasp that found its way to the beach this summer, a helicopter from an invading country, emboldened by a lack of predators; that house, with its splintery pine walls and its Joseph Cornell boxes of shells, is on that inner curve. It sits on a high promontory above the bay like a lookout station. From the small gray porch you can see all the way to Plymouth. It was on this hill that the Pilgrims first received corn from the Payomet people who lived here; there is a marker, a few miles away at High Head, where they discovered and drank from a spring. A friend to whom I recently recounted this history said, you must say: they *stole* the corn.

The beach we go to is on the ocean side, two miles away. When I went to the beach in June this year I was startled at how long the sun lasted over the dune; in August the sun slides out of sight by late afternoon. The light lasts longer by the water. In August in the afternoon, we move our towels closer and closer to the shore until we are almost in, but it is too cold to go in. It is almost always too cold to go in. It is bracing, the shock of the cold on the skin, but we persist— as if going in were an act of penance, an expiation, a test of character to appease the Puritans, their eyes watching us from the lost trees. When I was a girl I stayed in for hours, my lips turning blue, in my red serge bathing suit. Now my children wear wetsuits and swoop like herons on their surfboards, landing on shore only to turn their backs and go out again.

It is a mystery to me why I cannot think of this particular piece of geometry—the bay, the back shore, the straight line from Corn Hill to Plymouth, the High Head spring—without thinking of the Pilgrims. But there they are, in their funny hats and dark clothes, fierce, monkeylike, behind the scrubby trees. One day early in the morning I drove my husband down the last knuckle of the Cape to the airport at Provincetown—he had an appointment in New York. That half an hour after I left I would turn around, because he had forgotten not only his wallet but his keys, was indicative of the disorder we were entering then, that even now illegible year, though I did not at the time realize it, nor would I for many months afterward; these were warnings that even the firkins in the pines could have told me about.

After Truro, the second-growth forest of locusts and elms thins out. A millennia ago the glacier from the frozen sea, carrying rocks and earth, stopped just here, at High Head. The bluff it left rises one hundred feet, and at the bottom is the kidney shape of Pilgrim Lake, the glacier's afterthought. In good weather the lake reflects the sky. Beyond the lake, on the left, begins the string of Monopoly house cottages that front Provincetown Harbor. To me these had always looked cheerful. The houses I have known on the Cape are more elaborate: bigger, more entrenched in the dream of summer passed down from aunts and cousins, vested in the idea of permanence and perfection: the hurricane lamp, the curtain with its hokey pattern of seashells. They have room under their eaves for quarrels and reliquaries; even the less lived-in have hidden away matchboxes where mice have died and shrines made of small stones for buried butterflies. They are houses that have secrets and spit them out by accident. A friend of mine called the other day and told me that when he closed up his house this summer he opened a drawer and found a cache of writing paper from the magazine where his stepfather had worked for fifty years, imprinted with the magazine's first address, thirty years out of date, where he knew his stepfather had been happy. On a closet shelf in my mother's house on the Cape—a house with five bedrooms and a cellar that smells of damp, to which I am allergic—there is an old gray tennis ball. The day a few summers ago that the International Astronomical Union decided that Pluto was not, after all, a planet, the children found it at the foot of the dune. It had been washed up by the high tide. It looked like a fossil fallen from the sky. "It's Pluto!" someone said. I have been unable to admit that I am saving it, but whenever I return to that house I check a little anxiously to make sure that the zealous cleaning woman whom my mother employs, and who leaves notes like "Monday: dusted under the sink!" hasn't thrown it away.

So to me, the houses along Route 6, white as Chiclets,

rented—I always imagined—by the week by people, hoping
for sand and surf, for the charcoal barbecue, to "get away,"
seemed enviable, coming as I do from a tribe that when it
arrives on the Cape isn't getting away, but *getting to,* arriving at
a place with its own intricate maze of switchbacks, where the
person you were the summer before, in the same old shirt, and
the one before that, examines your soul for new stains. One
August, though, because some people we knew, on a whim—
because with one thing and another it had been an expensive
year, or maybe because the house they usually took in the
woods had been sold, or taken back by the owners for the
month because their niece was getting married at the Red
Inn, the usual course of why a house falls away, like a snail
shell—decided to rent one of those houses. They were lithe,
loose-limbed people. He was a musician, and she, to her chagrin, I think, the daughter of a senator, who taught in a Mon-
tessori school. In the looping, elliptical world of the Cape, they
were not really our friends, but friends of friends, who had met
them years ago when their children played Frisbee together on
the beach. Then, I want to say, as it turned out—but of course
it did not turn out at all, or if it did, for a while it turned out
badly—there was a connection between us. This woman's half
sister was the sister-in-law of my first husband's cousin. Or
something like that. This couple, though, were still not our
friends. They were the friends of friends . . . but there was a
link. Later, I would learn that there was bad blood between
the sister-in-law and the cousin, but that's another story, told
to me in the dusty Palm Court of the Plaza by a woman twice
my age, who knew them both, the week before the hotel was
closed. When I told my husband about these connections, at

first, and then when I learned more, his interest did not match mine. He is one of ten children while I am one of three—chess pieces in an endgame, sensitive to nuance, poised for conflict. To these kind of intimate coincidences he admits only a nodding acquaintance: better, to him, to be less known.

"Come by and see us!" they said, as we packed up one afternoon to leave the beach. Usually when we are in our house on Corn Hill we go nowhere, but I told my husband as we walked up to the car that I wanted to go; I had never been inside one of those houses. I had in my mind a vision of a simple bright room, an ur-room, with a table and three chairs, a tidy kitchen, two or three beds. A house unlike ours, with grit in the corners of the stairs and wet laundry on the railings. Like most visions this turned out to be only partially accurate. We went after dinner. It was midsummer so the sun was still bright in the early evening. They gave us directions. Off the shore road before the Mobil station we turned left toward the water. It was the third identical house on the right after the sandy parking lot, and the front of the house, with a door and two windows, faced the bay. It opened directly onto a small deck, about six feet wide. The deck was like the deck of a ship. At the end of it was the water.

The house was grotesque. There was nothing wrong with it except it was lit up like a light box and our faces and even the tanned faces of the children took on the waxen look of the dead. The sun in the room was so strong our bones shone through our skin. There were no curtains on the windows. Why aren't there curtains? I remember thinking, and their small heaps of belongings, things that although I didn't know them well I would have been able to identify as belonging to them (a watch, some necklaces, a beach towel), looked like leavings.

We stayed for a while on the deck with our drinks. The sun set over the harbor. When I went in to use the bathroom the front room was blood red. The children were disappointed that their children weren't there. They had gone, by themselves on the bus, to spend the day in Provincetown and weren't back yet, and their covert glances at each other—communicating that there was no circumstance in which they would have been allowed to do this—summed up all the ways in which we, as parents, were below regard. Then we left and returned to our musty house on the hill, with its damp bathing suits and bowls left in the sink, its own sunset.

So the morning when I drove my husband to the Provincetown airport we passed those houses, white as bleached fish vertebrae on the east side of the highway. On the right was the lake, flat as a drawing of a lake, and where the water ended were the Province Lands dunes. I dislike those dunes and, as always, as we passed, I doled out for myself, from an infinite store, a little dollop of horror. Years ago I had a friend who had a fascination with the dunes, and now and again he would convince me to walk out into them, to cross the two-mile expanse of sand as a prelude to a day on the beach. No matter how fine the day began, before we had walked more than a quarter of an hour the wind would come up, first in a series of slaps, and then insistently, hurling sand without ceasing into our faces. We always came equipped with handkerchiefs to put over our mouths, so that conversation, too, ceased, which in any case had consisted only of my friend's exclamations of pleasure over the scenic, barren beauty of the dunes: It looked like Africa, he would cry, did it not? Now and again he would take a bottle of water from his knapsack and hand it to me, and I would rip the bandanna from my face and gulp furiously.

Here and there on the undulating hills of sand were what looked like gnarled old roots, but were, instead, the top branches of scrub pine trees that had been covered over by the sand. My friend thought this was poetic. Imagine, he often said, the fossil of the tree, but to me this idea only deepened my distrust of the dunes and my feeling, quite apart from my annoyance at the wind, the pinpricks of sand, the grit, that in only a moment we too—or at least I, for I was certain my friend was too perspicacious for any calamity to befall him—would either be buried under the sand too, or lose my way.

Most people who walk in the dunes take a compass. I have never found it possible to read a compass; it skitters in my hands, a hot star, a Ouija board planchette. In the Province Lands, the dunes rise up and down twelve or thirteen feet, with declivities between them: the horizon is as elusive as a dream. I do not have a compass. If I ever had a compass, I am sure it was a Cracker Jack affair, a plastic prize from a children's birthday party, easily and inevitably lost. My friend—of course—had no need of a compass. Set down anywhere on earth, he knew, like a bird or an animal, exactly where he was, and navigated faultlessly, finding, in a city he had been to exactly once, a decade ago, at night, the bar where his uncle, now dead, had bought him a beer. I, on the other hand, can be lost even in my own city, the city in which I was born and where, now, I live only three blocks from where I lived as a child. Coming up out of the subway I try to hold in my mind the direction in which I was traveling when I left the train car and every so often I have to ask a passerby to point me in the direction I should be going. I find this vaguely humiliating, and reproach myself with visions of intrepid Victorian travelers, leaving Portsmouth with only a satchel, on their way to serve as governesses to the children of the Raj.

My friend had a compass nonetheless. It was a handsome one in a leather pouch which, when we were walking in the dunes, he sometimes consulted sagely. In the dunes, time, like the horizon, had little meaning. A few minutes can and does seem an hour. Even if we walked steadily in a straight line to the back shore, even if the wind—as it rarely was—was still, it seemed to me an age as long as the time since the Payomet walked with their arrows and chalk, before the water (which one moment ago was nowhere to be found) loomed like a cloud bank in the east, we unpacked our towels and sandwiches, and, still swathed in my gritty clothes, I began the endless debate about whether or not I would strip down to my bathing suit and go in.

The morning I drove to the airport I had not walked in the dunes for almost twenty years. The last time it was winter. It was New Year's Day. My friend, who by then was my first husband, had invited another couple to spend the weekend with us. It had snowed the night before, and the locust and pine trees that line the back roads were covered with frost. The trees on the Cape are small trees, because the high winds keep them from growing very tall, and the woods have the dollhouse proportions of a children's story. After lunch we drove to the shoulder of the highway near Pilgrim Lake, and began to walk to the sea. As usual, I had little interest in going. It was cold, for one thing. But our guests had been cajoled by the idea of this outdoor adventure: it was a wonderful way, everyone agreed, to begin the year. It was an arctic landscape. The sand, usually a very pale biscuit brown, was white. We were wearing warm hats and gloves and heavy shoes that sank into the snow, which wasn't very deep, an inch or two, and the lugs of the soles made marks on the snow. When we lifted up our feet we could see the cold sand. The tops of the strangled trees were black against the white, the limbs like ink drawings. As we walked, one of our friends, a Chinese historian, told us about a buried city in China: a sandstorm had crept over the city at night, and the only people who survived were the servants of the grandest houses, who slept under the eaves. Overnight, the city became a graveyard. The servants opened the painted shutters of the attics, climbed out, and walked over the buried houses and the hidden bodies of the dead. As we traipsed through the cold I imagined the light steps of the servants edging over the sand. It was springtime—I thought—in the Chinese city, and the people stood on the crest of the terrible wave of sand. It was a holiday. In the far distance from the top of the sand hill they could see another village, one not covered in sand, and they began to walk toward it, taking with them small things they could carry: vases and bundles of clothes.

It was windy. It began to snow again. The flakes came down softly at first, then harder. The wind which arrived with the snow began to twist and turn the flakes. Specters of snow, ghost white in the white landscape, began to follow us. No one else was distracted or concerned. They called to one another over the wind: Albert Pinkham Ryder had painted the beach in a snowstorm! The snow stung. It was impossible to see where we were. I had been tramping over the dunes a little behind the others.

On the two-lane highway into Provincetown the road curves slightly at the entrance to the Province Lands dunes. In the lay-by where we left our car that New Year's Day was a sign printed with the combination of welcome and warning that is usually found in wild places that have been domesticated. BRING OUT WHAT YOU BRING IN, the sign reads. WELCOME TO OUR FRAGILE LANDSCAPE. There is an illustration on the sign of a huge landmass festooned with ice, like a huge chunk of dirt a bulldozer might rip out of the earth to make room for a skyscraper, and beside it the legend reads THE LEGACY OF THE GLACIER.

Two of my children were in the back of the car, and I told them how exactly the same the landscape looked as when I was a little girl and drove with my mother to take my father to the Provincetown airport so that he could fly to New York. The other place I have seen a landscape that resembled it—the scrub and the rolling hills, and the places where the sand has worn away, leaving striations of clay the color of sulfur dioxide and ferrous sulfate—is in New Mexico, where recently a man who had once been and will probably be again the governor of Nambé Pueblo told me that he had found seashells in the dirt where he is irrigating, a thousand miles from the ocean.

What *am* I thinking? The landscape, the shells, the Nambé tribe who are not the Payomet of Corn Hill, the sense of trying to hold on, of trying to find a thread that will hold no matter how far it is unwound, zigzagging through the pines. When a friend of mine was small—is it part of the story that she is deaf, was born deaf, or not? what is and isn't part of the story?—her mother organized treasure hunts in the woods. Lines of string wound through the branches, and each child followed a string, which unspooled to a treasure: a little tin toy, a whistle, a compass. Is it part of the story that the woods behind the house were full of brambles? What does it matter that in New Mexico, in the mountains, you can find blue columbine and delphinium, their starry blossoms the exact color of the kettle ponds in Truro two thousand miles away?

The beach we go to is the most beautiful beach in the world. What can that mean? Who is *we*? This winter, because family life as I had known it seemed to be ending—the web of string stretching over the small forest, uprooting trees, as we looked for clues and treasure—I drove the route over and over again to Truro. If you get lost, go to the last place where you knew where you were, we told the children. We once found Rose in the butterfly house, covered with butterflies. *Don't move.* I hadn't spent a winter there for twenty-five years. The storms had so abraded the back shore that the dunes were cleft. It was as if the dunes, fighting back like Cuchulain, had become waves and were throwing themselves into the sea. I wasn't sure all that winter whether we would be able to go to that beach again. When we went to look in March—my daughter and her friend, an old friend and his children—the path down to the shore had caved in. But by May the town took itself in hand and trucked in sand to fill the gaps. In June we could walk single file down the steep slope, more than usually full of stones, to the beach.

Over and out. Later in the day, when my children and I get down to the beach—their father has his wallet, his keys, he has now landed in New York—we will spread out our towels, which are still slightly damp from the day before, which smell of salt. At a glance we know if the tide is coming in or out. The children will look for the break—the place they will paddle out on their surfboards to wait for waves. When they were small I spent every day in the summer counting heads. The girls wore the same bright bathing suits so I could see them in the water. When they were very small I spent the summer up to my waist in the water so that I could swim and fetch them out if they went under. In snapshots on the bookcases in New York the light around them shimmers. The light peers over the dunes, then disappears. I have sunspots on my right hand and on the right side of my face from sitting on the beach year after year in the late afternoon; at high noon it is as bright as the light in the house in Provincetown that so frightened me, a light without shadows. I wonder if I would be as frightened of it now.

When we are older perhaps the light is not as frightening, we are perhaps less interested in the past because the house that we carry around is ourselves. It is not as necessary to see ourselves everywhere; we have seen worlds upended and then slowly, gradually reconstitute themselves. In August, at the beach, my children will look for the break, and I will sit by the water at low tide pretending to read, looking up every few words from the page to find them in the water. When our friends come down the hill to the shore with their towels and bags of chips, with their car keys strapped to their beach bags to keep them from being lost in the sand—friends who rent other houses, under the trees—the first thing they will ask is: Are you going in?

Are you going in? Have you been in? Do you want to go in? A friend who is now dead—who lived in the woods that we love, too, the woods on the way to the beach, the trees that I picture wrapped in their web of string, gnarled, full of bayberries, the woods that have yielded their treasure—would say to us when we were young and unsure, yet surer than we are now, "You never regret a swim in the ocean or another child."

What is regret? I lost a house, one that I loved, we are going into the interior; inside a house of wattles is a tiny shell, on the shell is a sail, inside the walnut is the fairy-tale child. This is where I am now: DO NOT PASS GO, DO NOT COLLECT $200. When a child we know was very small and unhappy she was too little to play, she announced, *"The pink money is mine."* What is mine? When the children were younger they played Monopoly games that when it was raining went on for days, until someone tilted the board on purpose and the houses fell from the board. Are you the shoe, the dog, the rocking horse? Once I found a field mouse in a kitchen matchbox coffin, dry as a twig. When it stopped raining the children played at walkie-talkies under the window, tin cans attached by eight feet of string. *Can you hear me? Over and out.* Darning needles stitch the air. On our part of Long Nook Beach, the shelf splits off. A few steps and you are in the water. Are we going in? Where are we going and from where do we leave?

Mary McCarthy's Chest

O ne day many years ago at the magazine where I then worked, an envelope crossed my desk. It was an airmail envelope, the kind seldom seen anymore, but then it meant news from afar. The envelope was blue, like a scrap of sky. Chevrons, red and blue, marked the corners, suggesting a shot arrow, which in a way it was. The postmark was Paris. The letter was addressed to me. My name, and the address of the magazine, had been typed on a manual typewriter. The lines of the address were indented, one stepped under the other. It looked at once elegant and slapdash. For some reason this entranced me. The return address, typed in the upper left corner, was Rue ———, Paris. The sender was Mary McCarthy.

At that time I was working as an assistant in the Fiction Department. It was my second year at the magazine, and my second job there. Or, really, my third, if I count on my fingers. My first job, in the typing pool, had lasted three days. It had come about circuitously, almost haplessly, the way many things happened at the magazine, although I didn't, of course, know that then. But haplessly as a paper boat circling a pond is drawn by the current. I had graduated from college the year before, and after a certain amount of to-ing and fro-ing had returned to New York, where I was living in an apartment with a Dutch door and a leaky skylight over the bathtub. When it rained the tub was splotched with dark spots, as if a dog had shaken himself off on the cracked porcelain. The apartment was twenty-eight blocks south of the apartment where I had lived until I was five, and two blocks from the Soldiers' and Sailors' Monument, on Riverside Drive and Ninety-second Street. When I was a little girl I had walked with my father on a winter's day from our apartment to that monument, and that event—the long walk, the snow, my attempt to keep up with him, uttering no complaints—had become mythic in our family. After I had lived in that apartment for some years, it occurred to me that besides the low rent, and the fact that it had fallen into my lap, and the equal fact that it wasn't on what we then called "a drug block" because this was the eighties, and blocks near the park were either drug blocks, or not—was that it was as far as my journey from childhood could take me, as if that distance had been foreordained. I would lie in bed at night and try to imagine the house as it had once been. When I flicked at the marred whitewash on the wall with my fingernail, the blue and silver wallpaper rose up under the paint. Sometime during this period, of peeling the paint with my fingernail and peering up at the bathtub skylight, rereading Ngaio Marsh, I realized that I had almost no money at all, besides what my grandmother slipped into my pocket when I visited her in Chelsea, and I needed to get a job.

At that time the magazine was located in a large, nondescript office building on Forty-third Street. A number of years before, a writer affiliated with the magazine had made his way without touching the sidewalk from the office to the Chrysler Building, six blocks away, through a series of catwalks, overpasses, and tunnels: in the lore of the magazine this was viewed as an enviable, even emblematic, achievement, as then a reigning idea behind the magazine itself, implicit in its character, which reflected the life of its editor, was the primacy of secret routes and power of the inner life, which was viewed as an Escher landscape, with stairways that went nowhere, punctuated by moments of transcendence in which life, usually opaque, opened by means of a hidden switch. In the lobby there was a tobacconist, a dry cleaner, and a luncheonette.

The letter that I had written to "The Editor" requesting a job was not my first correspondence with the magazine. For over a decade, since I was twelve, I had been sending poems to "The Editors." These had been returned. Tucked inside the typewritten pages was a small note on good-quality paper, with *The New Yorker* colophon, a man with a top hat and a monocle. The paper hovered between yellow and ecru, and the colophon was black. The preprinted note thanked me for my submission, but regretted the impossibility of publication. I received forty-two of those notes. I kept them in a shoe box, which one way or another has disappeared. When I dropped the letter into the mailbox on the corner, I had no expectation of a reply; then, it seemed to me uncertain that any person actually worked there. This was before the Internet but not before celebrity; nonetheless the staff of the magazine, and its mysterious editor, were absent from the annals of people-watching. One of the most famous writers for the magazine had not been seen in public for almost twenty years. That this was caricature or simply an extension, played out to an extreme, of a policy I sensed I did not yet understand, nor of course could I know the effect this policy had, or would have on me, or on people that I loved. But there it was. The magazine seemed to emanate from a small, urbane, luminous planet vaguely resembling the planet belonging to Saint Exupéry's *The Little Prince* (again, this stab in the dark was not far wrong), in which people spoke courteously and often mirthfully to each other, and in which most of their shopping needs—for embossed neckties and fly-fishing rods—were catered to by shops which advertised, discreetly, in four-point type, in the magazine's back pages.

At that time there was no masthead or table of contents. Many of the articles, especially in what I was to learn was called the front of the book, were unsigned. There was a notion that these were written "by the magazine," as in "We were downtown the other day when . . ." If it was necessary for some reason that the article appear in the first person, the convention was "An old friend writes . . ." When, after a time, that person was sometimes me, this appeared as "A young woman we know writes . . ." When a writer's name did appear, it was in small block letters at the end of what was often a very long article, of thousands of words, so that generally, the reader discovered who had written the article only when he or she came to the end: verbosity offset by self-effacement. There were a series of sobriquets used by regular contributors to the magazine, which included the Long-Winded Lady and Our Man Stanley; these monikers were trumped, as it were, by a few that referred, consistently, to people who did not exist at all, among them Owen Kethery, the polite anagrammatic Beauregard who replied to letters sent to the editor (these did not appear in print). Thus, at the magazine's offices, there were writers who existed whose names did not appear, and others who did not appear but whose names appeared frequently, on letters that were typed and sent out into the U.S. Mail. For a short time, later, I was among those who typed them. This sense of unreality, in its most utilitarian sense, had applications outside the magazine: the ex-wife of the former editor of the magazine, a man mythically uncouth, whose exclamations of disbelief and irritation covered a steely sense of order, aesthetic and otherwise, owned a plant nursery in Connecticut, whose catalogues were studded with advice from one Amos Pettingill, who in my mind was a sort of imaginary brother to the imaginary Owen Kethery, himself a scion or nephew of the magazine's mascot, that fictive man in the top hat watching a butterfly through a monocle, whose name, I was to learn, was Eustace Tilley. A preponderance of Wildean vowels. In its less utilitarian incarnation, if unreality can be said to be utilitarian, this feeling of shifting identity—of not being quite there, wherever *there* was, of sidestepping not place but history, a refusal to *be pinned down,* or to sacrifice equivocation to the imperative—was mother's milk. Or, better, father's. There were always so many sides to an issue. The possibilities rose up, like empty cartoon bubbles over ten-point type, suggesting the unanswerable which was the only answer. Recently a writer whom I met at the magazine when I was twenty-three, and he was almost forty—he had been one of the first critics of the war in Vietnam—was talking over dinner about what had happened in Southeast Asia since he started reporting, for the magazine, as a very young man, in 1966. He said that, well, it had turned out exactly as he, or we—I don't remember whether he used "I" or "we," but it was probably the latter, as

he has retained the habit of not calling attention to himself—
had imagined it, but you know, *we could have been wrong. It
could have happened differently.*

The cover of the magazine—then, as now, a weekly—was
always a drawing or a painting by one of the magazine's art-
ists. There was no attempt whatsoever to advertise the current
contents. The font in which the magazine was printed was not
exactly black. It was almost, but not quite, ghost writing, the
kind of writing I had practiced as a child which my cousin
had taught me—the same cousin who, when I slept over her
house woke me up, and conducted séances in the middle of
the night, wearing a silk headscarf printed with stirrups which
I recognized as a castoff of her grandmother's. This writing,
with a special silver pen, was only truly visible if you shone a
flashlight directly on the paper.

I dropped my query letter, with a résumé, if it could be
called that, in the mailbox on the corner of Ninety-first Street.
In two days I had a reply. Such were the mails. Could I telephone Mr. Gibbs at ALgonquin 7-7500, to make an appointment? I could, and did. My appointment was for the day after
tomorrow, at 3 p.m. I later learned that Mr. Gibbs, who proved
to be a well-turned-out man of any age between forty and seventy (I had no way of judging, then, the age of anyone more
than a few years younger or older than myself), in addition to
fulfilling a job called managing editor, also reported on yacht-
ing, or anything at all having to do with boats. The magazine,
I would learn, reserved whole areas of inquiry for one writer
or another. These included but were not restricted to dance,
medicine, France, film, economics, law, fashion, presidential
inaugurations, New York City politics, golf, fly-fishing, corn,

visual art, England, theater, and outer space. This guaranteed exclusivity and was an attempt, I think, to eradicate rivalry; like many things at the magazine it had a familial aspect: so-and-so was "good at" baseball, or China, and his or her proclivities and/or talents were both thus applauded and constrained, a branch, or knob, on the family tree.

The afternoon of my appointment I made my way to Midtown. I took the subway. When I first arrived in New York in September—I liked to think of it as "back in New York," although my family moved to Long Island when I was five or six—the subway intimidated me. The year before I went to college, and the summer after my freshman year, I had had a job at a bookstore on Forty-seventh Street, shelving books—the bookstore was its own education, as the basement was not arranged in alphabetical order or by subject (although all the books were literary) but by circle, Lytton Strachey and Carrington, for example, were shelved together, and Lee next to Capote. It was also where I saw my first and only heroin overdose and fell in love with a boy a decade older, who lived in Harlem and who poured scotch into a carton of ice cream for breakfast. To get to the bookstore I took the train in from Long Island every day, and the subway uptown. My own father, I knew, had taken the subway or the trolley in Brooklyn alone from the time he was six: it was to me the equivalent of my grandfather's Russian tales of walking three miles in hip-deep snow to get to school—remote and inexplicable. In the seventies he used to say that he would never have married my mother then: she lived in the Bronx, and after a date he would take her home and then wait on the platform at midnight for the train to take him back to Brooklyn. "Now," he said, shaking his head, "I would have been killed." The subway was the stuff of family myth. In my grandparents' generation children went to work early (everything happened early—my grandfather and his younger sister had sailed alone on the *Philadelphia* from Minsk via Liverpool at ages five and three, respectively); there was the one great-aunt who had received a proposal from the man to whom she would be married for more than sixty years, when they met by chance on the subway after not speaking for a year, after a quarrel.

As usual, I arrived too early. I had spent time deciding what to wear, and had in the end decided on a burgundy tweed skirt my mother had made for me three or four years ago, hemmed at the knee, black tights, brown suede pumps, and a black cashmere turtleneck sweater, which I felt elevated the rest of it. It was April. I had realized as I walked from the subway that the hem of the skirt, which I thought looked appropriately "bookish" was frumpy in the extreme—by now it was too big at the waist but bunched on the hips—was coming down. By the time I arrived I was hot, and looked longingly at a girl about my own age going up in the elevator, who was wearing a loosely belted trench coat over blue jeans. I loitered by the shoe stand. It was too early for that, even, and I decided to walk around the block. This took too long, and I ended up late, staring with horror at the outsize clock with gold hands that presided over the lobby. I did not register that the lobby was peculiar in that it had five elevators, of which only one was manned, by an operator in livery, with white gloves. An automatic elevator came first, and I got into it. The letter, with its colophon of the top-hatted lepidopterist, had told me to arrive at the nineteenth floor. There must have been a receptionist,

in the small, boxed-in area by the elevator—there was a receptionist on each of the three floors the magazine occupied—who
unlocked the door, but I don't remember, now, who that was.

The door opened onto a barely furnished hall. In retrospect
it seems to me that it was the most aggressively nondescript
reception area I have ever seen. The wall immediately opposite
the door held a wood-frame couch with two flat, hard Nauga-
hyde cushions. These were brown. It was the sort of couch you
wouldn't be surprised to see cast off in the street. Adjacent
to this was an armchair, equally unpromising. There was a
hammered brass lamp with a stained shade on a gimcrack side
table, and across from the couch a small low table held two
magazines. One had a torn cover. They were both at least a
year out of date. The walls were painted the color of what I
thought of as "face powder," pinkish brown. Like powder, the
paint seemed to be flaking. I sat down on the couch, my knees
touching, my heels elevated in the uncomfortable pumps. It
was 1982, but I had been brought up in another universe, and
that universe at that moment came to the fore, slipping over a
lengthy, troublesome and headstrong adolescence and my current life—my tiny apartment on West End Avenue where I
stayed up too late, running the hot water into the bathtub
until it ran out, while someone sat on the ledge, smoking, and
talked to me. Recently, in an early book by Antonia Byatt,
I read the words "If I had been brought up by people who
made allowances, I would not have had to take so many," and
thought of myself then. A voice in my head said, "Nice girls
don't cross their legs," and so I sat, at the edge of my seat.

After about five minutes, Mr. Gibbs bounded down the hall
to collect me. He was wearing a navy blazer with gold but-

tons, a blue-striped shirt with a white collar, a navy twill tie, and gray flannels. He was fresh-faced, and looked so exactly in aspect like the White Rabbit that rather than smiling I felt a small shock that I recognized as fear. "Come, come," he said, and shook my hand. I followed him down one leg of the face-powder hall and then another, barely registering the curious fact that the mirror had been placed catty-corner where the corridor walls met, although I did catch sight of my own face in it. At the end of the second corridor, before we turned right into Mr. Gibbs's office, through the only open door I had yet seen, I saw a girl of about my own age, sitting in a dark room, at a large desk, illuminated by a gooseneck lamp. From a distance of about twenty feet I could see she had pale, sharply defined features, and she was wearing a fawn-colored crewneck sweater. Beyond her, over her right shoulder, was a closed door. Her copper hair shone in the light. She was on the phone, and she was making a little comical face at the receiver. When our glances met, she gave me a conspiratorial look and nodded her head, slightly. Mr. Gibbs held the door to his office open, and I walked through it. Half an hour later, when I left, the desk was empty, the light out, and I wondered if I had imagined her.

Mr. Gibbs, who was called Tony but whose given name was in fact Wolcott, was kind to me. The interview had a practiced air. The room was almost blindingly light after the hall and the sepulchral room I had glimpsed. One wall, as I remember it, was windowed. The office itself was cluttered with books and folders and littered, on every surface, with what I would learn to call galleys. These were sheets of mimeographed paper, in which articles that would appear, either next week,

next month, next year, or never, were set up in the magazine's ghostly type, and then were reread and revised without
end. Most of the galleys I saw had small blue sheets of paper
clipped to them, on which writing, small as a snail's trail, took
up a good deal of space. Mr. Gibbs sat me down in a captain's
chair with the emblem of the college we had both attended
painted on it, and asked me, genially, what I thought I might
do at the magazine if I stayed for five years. I had no idea. Five
years to me was an unfathomable length of time. I believe I
muttered something about "being a writer." He nodded as if
he understood all that. My résumé, such as it was, was in his
hand. I had been the poetry editor of a slightly dégagé college publication, which we printed on newsprint paper, and
I had worked at the bookstore. During college I had been a
waitress. He folded this piece of paper in half, and picked up
the telephone. A few words were exchanged, among them the
name "Harriet," and "five minutes." At the close of this cryptic
conversation, Mr. Gibbs got up and it was clear I should do so
too. I was acutely aware of my drooping hem. We walked back
down the face-powder corridor, passing the terrible sofa, the
brass lamp, and the torn magazines. The hall zigzagged. At
the end of it Mr. Gibbs handed me over to a woman with reading glasses around her neck, a pencil skirt and a sweater, and
a comfortable look of extra upholstery about her. Her hair was
steady in 1940s curls, and she introduced herself as Harriet
Walden. Her accent was southern, with an overlay of Rosalind
Russell in *His Girl Friday.*

It transpired that I was to take a typing test. I blanched.
I was a terrible typist. We entered a room in which five or
six manual typewriters sat on an equal number of desks. The

room was empty. The idea, as Mrs. Walden put it, was to see what I could do. *Nothing,* I thought to myself, bitterly. She ushered me into a small, glassed-in cubicle in the corner of the room—it was obviously her station. To the right of the desk was a music stand, on which she put a copy of *Naked Lunch,* by William Burroughs. It was a book I had once tried to read; I'd failed.

"Have a go at that," she said.

She put a sheet of paper into the typewriter, and put a little stack of paper by my side. Then she departed. I looked despairingly at the text, and began to type. There was a large clock in the office but I didn't look at it. The words, clumsily, sprang up under my fingers. About five minutes later Mrs. Walden poked her head in. I stopped typing. She pulled the sheet of paper out of the typewriter. I wanted to put my head in my hands. To my surprise, she slowly ripped the piece of paper into strips. She looked me up and down. I felt sorry about the hem. I tried to stand up straighter. She looked directly into my eyes, and said, "Well, you *sound* like a typist.

"I'll be in touch, of course," she said.

She walked me down the corridor, past another catty-corner mirror. I asked if I could use the ladies' room and she directed me—it was beside the elevator. I washed my hands, and looked in the mirror. In the mirror-view, behind me, there was a half-open door, in an alcove set apart from the toilet stalls. I wondered, idly, if there might be a shower, and I imagined myself, transformed, going out to dinner after work, in a cocktail dress. I had never owned anything remotely resembling a cocktail dress (the only dress I owned then had been made out of red-striped Mexican cloth, and my brother had told me I looked like I was wearing a bedspread, at which he had snickered). The dress I had on in my imagination, I realized with chagrin, was a blue silk dress that belonged to my mother, and I dismissed it. Instead, gazing at my reflection without looking at it—a technique I had perfected to avert despair—I thought about the ratty couch, and William Burroughs, and the man in the monocle who liked butterflies, and my shoe box of rejection letters, and I admitted to myself what I had known since the moment I stepped off the elevator: for reasons I could not explain, even to myself, I wanted to be in this place more than I had ever wanted anything in my life. I desperately hoped that Mrs. Walden would call. I felt desperate about the desperation, because I knew that I would now spend the next few days barely venturing out of my apartment, should I miss a call. I thought, fleetingly, of the girl under the gooseneck lamp, and wondered if I would see her again. Then I descended nineteen floors to Forty-third Street, and the shoe shine stand. The next day Mrs. Walden called me. If it wasn't too much trouble, could I come to work the following Monday at ten o'clock? The salary, she said apologetically, was $13,285. I sensed that she was apologetic not about the figure, exactly, but at the idea of having mentioned money at all. Mr. Gibbs would answer any questions I might have. I accepted at once.

My first few days at the magazine occurred in a kind of trance. I had been given a job in the typing pool. The typing pool, which in my mind should be capitalized, as names of places are—Lethe or Gongora—the Typing Pool—as it was a place on the map of the magazine of both literal and psychic dimensions, was run by Mrs. Walden, who had been employed by the magazine for thirty-five years: by the time she left she had been there for more than half a century. She had been the personal secretary to the magazine's first editor. The force of her own considerable personality, charm, and common sense were laced with almost mandarin tact—of which she needed a great store, dealing, as she did primarily, with writers. Regarding the magazine, she had an encyclopedic memory. She had an incurable fondness for all the typists she hired. It was—I was to learn, slowly—the way that a good percentage of the female staff had entered into the magazine's circle dance: she functioned as a sort of benign Charybdis, and out of the typing pool had emerged many of the magazine's fact-checkers, editors, and writers. At her memorial service a number of years ago, one woman, now in late middle age, told a story in which, as a girl in the typing pool, she was presented with a manuscript by a notoriously difficult writer which was completely illegible: it was written in gobbledygook. Questions were generally addressed to the writer, but this writer had apparently lost his mind. (This was a circumstance which had been addressed before, but the signs were usually more gradual.) Silently, she handed the manuscript to Mrs. Walden, who put on her reading glasses and gazed at it intently. Then she smiled, encouragingly. "Oh dearie," she said. "Just type as written, but move your hands one key to the right."

The job of the typing pool was to type manuscripts. When I arrived at the magazine these were typed, in the main, on manual typewriters, as they always had been. On busy days, the typing pool was a noisy place. Generally, a manuscript would be submitted to the typing pool after the editor of the magazine had read it. The editor's name was William Shawn. He was invariably referred to as Mr. Shawn. In other cases

though, particularly when the writer was a longtime contributor to the magazine, or what I learned was called a staff writer,
these manuscripts would be handed to Mrs. Walden by the
writers themselves, full of cross-outs and overwriting, by hand,
between the lines, at the bottom and top of the page, and with
arrows pointing to other sections, or the back of the page, or
to other pages which would be connected by the writer's own
hieroglyphs. Mr. Shawn read these once they were typed.

Because it was clear that typing manuscripts of any length
was beyond me, I was set to work typing Mellecker letters.
These were the different types of rejection letters that were
returned with almost all the submissions that arrived in the
mail of "Fact" or "Reporting" pieces. There were twelve versions, which ranged from encouraging notes to, most often,
brief regrets (the phrase was "not quite right for us"); editors
who read the submissions would paper clip a slip with a number scribbled on it to the manuscript. They were called Mellecker letters because a real person, Miss Mellecker, signed
them. I was also put to work typing summations, written out
by hand, of ideas for stories for the section in the front of the
magazine called "Talk of the Town." These also emanated
from Miss Mellecker's office. They were about one hundred
and fifty words apiece, and were gleaned from the deluge of
press releases that were sent to the magazine's mail room each
week. Miss Mellecker sorted these and wrote the summations.
These were then typed and mimeographed, and a set of them
was available in Miss Mellecker's office, and in the "second"
office outside of Mr. Shawn's office, for writers to peruse. I
would learn that only very few of these press releases resulted
in stories: most of the story ideas were generated by the writ-

ers themselves; the best of these, according to the ethos of the magazine, were ideas that could not be summarized at all, that couldn't be pitched, because the story was simply something that happened, that the writer noticed and felt like talking about; it would be impossible to know what he thought about it, beforehand, and even *during,* until it was written: it was the *writing* that happened.

None of this was talked about. The Mellecker letters were typed on canary-yellow "seconds" paper: "Oldest Garbage Scow Retired from Active Use" or "First Annual Steel Drum Festival" or "Bagel Store Celebrates One Hundred Years." There was a small-town feel to these missives. The magazine inside its flocked urbanity retained a small-town incredulity about New York: a kind of "looky-here" that was at once put on, and not. One of the magazine's writers who had helped to establish this tone of voice had in fact found it almost impossible to live for any stretch of time in New York, and with his wife, a fiction editor whom many believed really ran the magazine, had decamped decades ago to rural Maine, where bundles of galleys and proofs arrived daily and returned with the aura of sea air and manure on them. This writer was also the author of three children's books. In two of them, animals who could not speak (a pig and a swan) were saved by writing, and in the third, a man who is born a mouse escapes from Manhattan in pursuit of a broken heart. (Many years later my children, all in turn, were entranced by these books; I found increasingly that I could not read them aloud without crying, and their father, who could trumpet like a swan but was not a writer, took over.) His wife, an avid gardener, wrote a column which was, among other things, about reading seed catalogues: the best garden, it seemed to go without saying, was the imaginary garden in the mind, in winter. Among the writers were extreme cases of the magazine's contrapuntal gait, the sidestep, a refusal to be quite *in line.* A recurring subject was wandering around, often by a "far-flung correspondent." There was no place the writer wasn't a tourist, incredulous even—crucially—at home. Or in time; regular clockwork, calendar time. A friend we knew wrote, in the magazine, about her refusal to own a working timepiece: at the end of the piece her mother tells her that if she does not buy a clock, she will blow up her house. That in the end that was what happened to the life we knew—that an almost brutal recalcitrance to tell time became itself a time bomb—was then remote.

There was almost no one at the magazine then, I knew by instinct, who had not been the wistful one out in the schoolyard, the one with one fast friend, trying to get Boo Radley to come out of the house. The press release about the bagel store came back, predictably, with a note in the editor's snail track handwriting, always in pencil, as if committing to ink would be going too far: not for us, he thought, perhaps next year. What does it mean to be always *just off,* to make a point that the point isn't the point? (As I write I am trying to fit in, somewhere, that from what I can find, almost no one who wrote for the magazine during that time, including those of us who are still alive now, has a Web site—that such an idea, of putting oneself forward, runs counter to *participating in ordinary time.*) Hopeless to imagine otherwise, really, because what might seem, now, like possible alterations we could have made in how we thought of ourselves, ways we could have gone *this way* instead of going *that way* into a sort of purdah—how it

could have happened differently—were foreign to the place
we literally found ourselves: the face-powder halls, the ladies'
lavatory with the glimpsed door, which it took me only a day
or two to discover contained a cot, with a pillow tucked into a
freshly laundered pillowcase and a folded blanket, for anyone
who, as the morning wore on, felt that they had to lie down
in a dark room.

I lasted three days in the typing pool. On the morning of
the fourth day Mrs. Walden called me into her office. In the
magazine's barely decipherable patois, delivered sotto voce,
and in a faint tone of apology, for unnameable fates at work,
forces beyond our control—there was at that time a kind of *Star
Trek* feel to the office, in which a butterfly net, pith helmet,
good manners, and lucid prose would suffice to keep the forces
of evil at bay—she told me that there had been a change in
circumstances. I was sure I was being fired. It turned out,
instead, after some circumlocution, that I was being asked if I
would consider, even remotely, being moved from the typing
pool. Would I mind, instead, working for Mr. Shawn? I was
perched on a chair with a rush seat (much of the furniture at
the magazine's office, like the couch by the elevator, seemed
to consist of castoffs from summer houses that had been sold
to pay taxes, combined with the most utilitarian kind of office
furniture, metal desks, and old file drawers that stuck and had
to be cajoled back on track. I was about to become intimately
familiar with the latter). The rush pricked the backs of my
legs. I was wearing tights, and I could feel a run starting. Since
my arrival at the magazine, I had seen Mr. Shawn once, at the
elevator. I had happened to be waiting with Mr. Gibbs, whom
I had not seen since my interview, and he had introduced me

to a small, elderly man, with a pink face and an air of extraordinary cleanliness, wearing an overcoat and a gray suit. I had noted the overcoat. It was a warm day in early May. That spring, Mr. Shawn must have been about seventy. Mr. Gibbs told him my name, and explained my presence by saying that I was "helping Mrs. Walden in the typing pool." Mr. Shawn nodded. He turned on me a look of extraordinary kindness tinted with resignation. Then he blushed. I understood, suddenly, that he was shy. Without holding out his hand, he murmured that he hoped I would be happy at the magazine. An elevator arrived, and Mr. Gibbs and I stepped into it. I made a move to hold the "open" button so that Mr. Shawn would not be left behind, but Mr. Gibbs gave an almost imperceptible shake of his head, and the doors closed behind us. The thought crossed my mind that perhaps Mr. Shawn was waiting for someone. I didn't think to question how Mr. Gibbs knew this.

In her office, Mrs. Walden had kept on talking, without a pause in which I could make a suitable response. She must have picked up the phone or made a prior arrangement, for the door to her office opened and a girl about my age came in. Mrs. Walden's own murmur, like lake water lapping at stones, stopped. She sighed and gave the girl a grateful look. "Here's Alice," she said. "She'll *explain* it to you."

It was the girl with copper hair. Mrs. Walden made a fluttering gesture with her hands. It was a signal to go. If I had known that this was the end, really, of falling under Mrs. Walden's gentle aegis, I probably would have clutched at her. As I got up, the ladder climbed up my tights. When we were outside Mrs. Walden's office I gestured to it ruefully. The girl shrugged. An acceptance and even expectation of indignities and inconveniences—laddered tights, late trains, muddles of all sorts—was part of the ether I had entered, though this was not yet known to me, nor was the convention of addressing these incidents, by translation, in a kind of Esperanto, with the catchall phrase, equal parts literal and ironic: "Onward and Upward." This tag occurred in ordinary conversation as well as the "header" for various articles, "Onward and Upward with the Arts," "Onward and Upward in the Garden," and so on. It was possible to rise above anything. "Well," said the girl, who up close I saw had fine, almost translucent skin and a piercing gray-green gaze, *"Obviously,* I'm Alice."

It was lunchtime and again, the typing pool was empty. In three days I had noticed that the pool operated in two kinds of time, in which things either had to be done immediately or in a kind of lurch and go. We perched on two hard schoolroom chairs. The news was not altogether good, but it was delivered in a voice of trenchant sanity, which was an almost physical relief after my wandery conversation with Mrs. Walden. The job I was being offered was as "second assistant" to Mr. Shawn. This job consisted of sitting in the office where I had first seen Alice illuminated by the gooseneck lamp. No one, I learned, wanted this job. This was because the second assistant's direct superior was a woman, J——, who was a bully. She was domineering, patronizing, contrary, and rude to almost everyone who tried to see Mr. Shawn, and it was the second assistant's job to placate them. J—— was obsequious, however, to the writers she was afraid of. These were writers who, for one reason or another, had a special relationship to Mr. Shawn.

Alice had been in the job for three weeks. The previous girl had quit and returned to Mrs. Walden and the typing pool. Alice was now slated to work in the Books Department. This was run for mysterious reasons by the magazine's theater critic, a termagant with an acerbic wit and very little patience. A few years later when I began reviewing books and I made an attempt to enter the book room to see what had come in, she would turn on me with a glare, "Don't even *think* of poking around." That afternoon a book that I had wanted to review, but hadn't mentioned to her, would land on my desk. But that was later. I poked at the ladder in my tights and made it worse. "Don't *do* that," said Alice.

I took the job. As Alice had promised, at the beginning at least, it was terrible. It was worse, I think, for me than it was for Alice, because her family, I had gleaned, had something to do with the magazine. What, exactly, was unclear, and I didn't like to ask her. Her aunt, or was it her cousin, I learned, was an editor in the Fiction Department. Or something. Subtly, this protected her from J——'s worst excesses. J—— was a small, large-bosomed woman with glossy black hair that she wore slicked back in a stiff ponytail. She favored cinched belts, patent-leather handbags, and high heels, which was a blessing because when she got off the elevator I could hear her, *click-clack, click-clack,* coming down the hall, a warning to me to be on guard.

My job was to answer the phone, type letters, file both incoming and outgoing mail (carbon copies were kept of all Mr. Shawn's correspondence, some of which, inexplicably, years later, was dumped into the East River), and fetch Mr. Shawn's lunch. Under no circumstances could Mr. Shawn be left alone to answer the phone or receive visitors. He did, I would learn, have a private phone line he answered himself.

On Tuesdays, I was also responsible for what was termed the "Talk" call. For this I went around to almost all the writers who had offices downstairs, on the eighteenth floor, and inquired, after knocking, and poking my head around the corner, whether they might have any "Talk." There were perhaps twenty or so offices on the eighteenth floor and I knocked on the door of any writer who might remotely be thinking of writing "Talk of the Town" that week. At the beginning I carried a list: some of the writers on it wrote "Talk" almost every week, but others had not contributed a "Talk" piece for years. The idea was that if they were not asked, they might be offended. (Conversely, I see now, it must have been torture for writers—some of whom had not produced any writing at all for months or even years—to have me brightly poke my head around the door every Tuesday.) The deadline for "Talk of the Town" was 4 p.m. If the writer had implied that he might be writing a "Talk" piece, I then went back by 3:45 to collect it, often waiting in a chair, after the writer had scooped off hats, blazers, mufflers, and collections of old proofs dating back several years, while he or she typed furiously. There was a big clock in the hall on the eighteenth floor. A few years later when I had an office there, the ticking of the clock on Tuesdays hounded me. (In 1991, when the last remnants of the magazine as we had known it were disbanded, and the offices moved across the street, I rescued the clock from a Dumpster; it now hangs in my kitchen above the pantry door, its work of reproach seemingly never over, *late, late, late:* for school, for the train, for whatever I was trying to accomplish that was just out of reach, an eternal deadline dream, above the boxes of cereal and pasta. My children learned how to tell time on it.)

The next morning I distributed the printed "Talk" galleys to all the offices on the eighteenth and nineteenth floors. Usually I slipped them under closed doors: not many writers arrived by 10 a.m. There were no set hours for writers. They were either in their offices, or not. Some offices had been locked, dust sheathing their particular haul of cast-off furniture, for years. One writer, a man then in his sixties, had been the magazine's Asia correspondent for decades. He was often out, of course, but one morning when I was delivering "Talk" his door was open. "Talk?" I said, apologetically. He asked me my name. I told him, and he then asked me how old I was, and how long I had been at the magazine, and where I had gone to school. I was too young to feel that the questions were impertinent; I was only a few years, after all, away from the questions which children are asked perpetually: How old are you? What grade are you in? What's your favorite subject? When I answered the last question he leaned back in his chair and smiled. He said, genially, "You look like Radcliffe girls are supposed to look."

I had very little to go on, to interpret this remark. For a moment I thought, wildly, of Ali MacGraw in *Love Story*. I felt, vaguely, that I should reject it as inappropriate and chauvinistic. This seemed, then, however, beside the point. To a large degree, the magazine existed in a world that predated the one in which I had marched in college, holding up a banner that said TAKE BACK THE NIGHT, listening endlessly to a boy I knew who wished he could be a lesbian. Entering its portals, I had in some way slipped backward in time. *Nice girls don't cross their legs.* It was a world I knew. When my mother took the train from Long Island into New York, she called it "going to town." In her top drawer was a box of white gloves that smelled faintly of Shalimar. The magazine still employed a switchboard operator. The *New Yawka,* she said, answering it. In my imagination, it was a world in which I felt at home. It behooved no one to flail at what was, in the end, I thought then, inconsequential, and I did not know then about the consequences of different kinds of silence that came out of compartmentalizing, the Joseph Cornell box filled with shells and tiny figurines, good manners which contained and hid a kind of violence. *Shut the door after you,* he said. I left, thinking that at least I looked like *something.*

What was it about the straws? I find, trying to remember, that I can't recall whether I was supposed to take the paper off half of the straw, without touching the straw itself, and then hand it to Mr. Shawn, holding the paper end, or the reverse. It must have been the former because I know I was not supposed to touch anything directly. The straw was on a tray, with a small carton of milk. I don't remember, either, what kind of sandwich was on the tray, or if it was a sandwich or a small carton of cottage cheese. Later, Mr. Shawn occasionally took me out to lunch, at the Algonquin or more usually the Oak Room at the Plaza, where he would have some soup and saltines. I know now that because often he would need to eat two dinners at two different apartments at the end of the day, he paced himself at lunch, but then it seemed of a piece with his cold weather gear—muffler and overcoat—in all but the hottest weather; the air of otherworldliness and mystery, in which the coat, too, emphasized Mr. Shawn's vulnerability.

He was sensitive to cold, to germs, and was afraid of enclosed spaces. I learned that the single elevator operator was kept on by the building's management expressly on Mr. Shawn's behalf. This was the reason he did not go down in the elevator with Mr. Gibbs and me; he was afraid of automatic elevators. He was afraid of traveling over bridges, and of flying. This meant that he depended, entirely, for his knowledge of the world—after about the age of thirty—on the writers who were his eyes and ears. When he left the city in the summer he ventured only as far as Bronxville, a few miles north of the office, from which he was driven into the city every day in a town car, because he did not drive. This vulnerability—linked to an inability to *deal,* to *feeling overwhelmed*—was in radical opposition to the magazine's Bunyanesque mantra "Onward and Upward," and was twinned with an equal admiration for derring-do high jinks (by trapeze walkers, fire-throwers, bartenders, presidents). A result was that the magazine was, among other things, a Festschrift of stories told to allay fear—of silence, of enclosed spaces, of the open road, of secrets. As Leontes says in *The Winter's Tale,* "Your actions are my dreams." There were many complaints, for example, about J——. The general feeling was that he could not know, for if he did, he wouldn't allow it. I think, though, that he did.

M r. Shawn figured in the dream life of almost every writer at the magazine. (In one of my dreams he appeared in his overcoat and muffler inside a huge transparent egg.) Mr. Shawn had started at the magazine as a writer but had sacrificed that career when he was needed to run the magazine; the implications, as far as they went, were clear. Mr. Shawn liked jazz; at the piano, as his son Allen has described it, he "let himself go and became another person." The syntax of the magazine was syncopated. Its notation was punctuation: a confetti of commas, em dashes, semicolons, and parentheses. There were things that could only be said *by the way.* (These were often the most important things.) This punctuation emphasized pauses, explanatory remarks, and exposition of ideas that seemed to be leading in one direction, until a curve ball whizzed past—a tiny meteor that appeared and fizzled to lie inert at the end of the sentence like any old rock, but that glittered if you cut it open. It was the *looky-here,* which showed up, not coincidentally, in the vernacular speech of the writers closest to Mr. Shawn, whose conversation was studded with "gee," and "no, really?" It was characterized by an elliptical, diffident half-stutter and a tone of wonderment that conferred genius on the person addressed, who felt himself truly answered, although it was possible and even predictable to come away not knowing quite *what had been said.* It gave rise to reading tea leaves: *Was I being fired? No, I have a new assignment.* This speech, in turn, influenced the cadence of the magazine which Mr. Shawn edited, word by word, to ensure natural diction: diction, that is, which corresponded to the way people around him spoke.

I was familiar with this patois because it was the language I myself spoke. I had learned it reading Elizabeth Bowen, Sylvia Townsend Warner, William Maxwell, and J. D. Salinger, who each spoke a version of it. When I'd come across these writers in the trance of reading in which I'd spent my adolescence, I had no idea that these stories had first appeared in the magazine, nor that William Maxwell had been the fiction editor there for many years, and if I'd been told it would have held no interest. Later, in school, I fell in with a group who spoke in similar elliptical circles, in which the minutiae of everyday life and especially every slight was treated as a worry stone or talisman—some of this was enhanced by marijuana—and when I arrived at the magazine I was living with someone who was an expert at this type of dream-talk. In my walk-up apartment we listened to Brian Eno and Lou Reed. We stayed up all night and in the morning we got into our grown-up clothes and headed for the subway. (He was working at another magazine, whose subject was what used to be called "hard news." The transition from the night spent talking on the side of the bathtub, the water cooling as I watched him blow smoke rings that eddied up to the cracked skylight, to workaday life was harder for him. It was less hard for me because the magazine was to some extent the element I breathed anyway, but this would prove harder, for me, in the end.)

It was only a few weeks into my tenure working for Mr. Shawn that I began to feel I had stumbled into a version of the Glass family, a sort of never-ending extended family reunion. In the magazine's library, on the eighteenth floor, there was a heavy, black-bound scrapbook for each writer: everything he or she had written which had appeared in the magazine was neatly pasted, column by column, onto oaktag pages. I had walked into the pages of a book that mirrored other books, Edward Eager's last story, *Seven-Day Magic,* in which the children discover that the book they are reading is a story about themselves and changes according to which child is reading it.

This was part of the impossibility of pinning anything down. I sat at the desk illuminated by the gooseneck lamp, and tried to piece things together. During the course of the day, a staggered parade of people, mainly writers who worked on the eighteenth floor, would end up by my desk and ask to see Mr. Shawn.

Of these people, only a few of them simply knocked on his door and walked in. Though I find it incredible now to imagine this conversation, within a day or so of my tenure, J—— told me who was permitted to do so (all but one or two of the names were then unfamiliar) and that I was expected to remember this. In retrospect, it was one of the only straightforward conversations I had in that office. The people who understood, who knew, that they could knock and enter were, in the main, writers between thirty and forty who had either gone to school with or were beloved by Mr. Shawn's elder son, or, in turn, related by blood or marriage to him or by some other, complicated arrangement. His son was an actor and writer, although none of his writing, which tended toward the scatological, had ever appeared in the magazine. To some extent, these particular writers had grown up inside the family life of the Shawns, which occurred in their apartment, on Fifth Avenue (among these writers, as it would turn out, were George W. S. Trow, Veronica Geng, Kennedy Fraser, Ian Frazier, Jamaica Kincaid, and Jonathan Schell). Editors at the magazine tended to send Mr. Shawn notes. (There was, of course, no e-mail. Mr. Shawn had his own blue memo pads, on which were printed RETURN DIRECTLY TO MR. SHAWN.) If a writer did not fall into this group he made an appointment. One exception to this rule was a writer in her sixties who arrived in the office almost every day with her dog, Goldie, with whom Mr. Shawn had been involved, in a kind of second marriage, at that time for over thirty years. By the time I was sitting at that desk, this had been publically acknowledged, in that Mr. Shawn's two sons had been told about it, five years before, when they were thirty-five and thirty years old, respectively. (His wife, Cecille, apparently, knew about it almost from the start.) Even now, typing these words, I feel a kind of miasma setting over me, like fog, or smoke rings, which you never see people you know blowing anymore, but then were a usual thing, the enactment of show-offy boredom. For *who cares,* really, that Mr. Shawn had a love affair that lasted for forty years, until his death? I find increasingly as I write I am resorting to words like "sort of," and "kind of," and "even," which represent my sense of *missing the point,* or the *impossibility of getting close to the truth.* Can I let that go for a moment here?

Also on the short list was a very young man my own age who appeared at my desk one afternoon in late June. He was extremely tall, with a high, fresh complexion, black hair cut short that made a V on the top of his head, and large, exophthalmic green eyes. He was dressed in a t-shirt and dungarees and looked as if he were going out to play catch. As a ten-year-old, he had chased fire engines in his hometown, in hopes of getting a story. His fingers were hitched into his belt loops. "He in?" he asked, with a nod in the direction of Mr. Shawn's closed door.

I nodded. The boy in front of me seemed to be a sort of apparition. He knocked on the door, and disappeared. When he came out about fifteen minutes later he said, "I have to go see some fireworks. Want to come?"

He had graduated from college a few weeks ago, and had come to New York because Mr. Shawn had asked him to. He had been editor of *The Harvard Crimson,* and had been hired over the telephone to write "Talk of the Town," which he was doing. He was having a grand time. When he was a little boy he had come with his family to New York for the first time. They had stayed in a hotel near Times Square, and from the window you could see the Marlboro Man blowing smoke rings. He stayed up all night at the window, enraptured. What does it mean that I know that? It means I loved him. Because Bill, at that time, represented just by being there, of having been chosen by Mr. Shawn—a bolt from the blue, for both of them—an attempt to move away from the hush, the silence that opened at the end of sentences, the portmanteau of secrets, in favor of the clear sentence, the uncomplicated *looky-here.* Bill resembled, in those days, Jimmy Stewart in *Mr. Smith Goes to Washington,* which is what, later, in fact, he became, a man bent on saving the world, who would build a global effort against climate change, 350.org, to bring attention to the proper carbon output without which we will all perish from the earth (or as he calls it Eaarth, a new name for a new place), which became another talk of the town, so to speak. But that is getting ahead of things, to how things *turned out,* things which could have turned out *some other way.*

M*r. Shawn's voice on the phone.* Before getting into that, it's important to note, I think, that it was a rule at the magazine (this was, in fact, told to me as a rule, by J——) that you never asked any writer, at any time, what he or she was "working on." It was also a rule, I learned, that writers never spoke about "their work." To speak was to risk "losing it"—the shoot of an idea would wither if exposed. At the center of the thought was that the particular gifts of some writers would appear only if the writer were *utterly left alone,* a desirable circumstance that was to some extent, I think, at the center of Mr. Shawn's own dream life, one in which a writer, with Mr. Shawn's quiet support, became a sort of Little Prince or St. Augustine, an Errol Flynn; Jack Nicholson in *Five Easy Pieces.* (A peril of this method is the risk of not being able to play the piano anymore.) Some at the magazine successfully turned their thoughts into type every few weeks, or months; others mulled things over without producing anything at all for years and existed, as far as I could tell, then, in a semi-ghostlike state, occasionally drifting around the office like haints; one of these was a writer whose sobriquet was the Long-Winded Lady, who for a time took up residence and slept on the cot in the ladies' room. The overall effect of this in the office was a kind of echolalia. It was also acknowledged that writing was so difficult, *getting it right* so taxing, that it was completely acceptable not to be able to write anything at all. But what it meant was that the working lives of writers at the magazine were almost totally interior—this is true, of course, of writers in general—and that the idea that what was most important was what was never spoken about eddied into peculiar and perhaps (but only in hindsight) predictable tributaries in which other things were not talked about, either. When a writer finished a piece, whether it was the work of a few weeks, or a decade (these were never called articles, or columns, but always pieces as if they were pieces of a giant puzzle that was gradually being put together over time, or a piece, as part of a recital program, and in a way, both of these things were so), it was handed to Mr. Shawn. Then came the wait, for the call.

As I write this I want to make clear that the lunacy of this was apparent, even then; not the protocol but the reaction to it: *we knew.* In order to distract themselves, writers cleaned their closets or made scenes with people they loved or got drunk, or any number of a hundred things in order to not think about it. Writers who were waiting for the call did not go out of the house, or were late for dinner parties, or left numbers where they could be reached. I do not know if Mr. Shawn had any inkling of this. Some writers swore that they could tell when the telephone rang whether or not Mr. Shawn was on the end of the line. Later, when I was waiting for a call from Mr. Shawn, I subscribed to this theory. If Mr. Shawn did not like the piece, if it "didn't work," that was the *end of it* (I don't remember an instance in which a writer took a piece that had been rejected and submitted it somewhere else); the taut nerve endings waited for the release of the phone call with a tension that was almost if not quite sexual. The relationship was triangular; it was between the writer, the page, and Mr. Shawn. The voice at the end of the line (it was a *line,* this was before even cordless telephones) was both hook and fish. It was wavery, ghostly, infinitely polite. It sounded like a voice coming from far away, perhaps the inside of a seashell. The phone call always began with the pretense that you didn't know exactly who was calling or what it might be about. Because Mr. Shawn worked at all hours of the day and night, reading manuscripts, it wasn't uncommon for the call to come at eleven thirty, or midnight, by which time the writer had lost hope entirely.

Because no matter what, he knew that the piece he had written was terrible.

In my first weeks of sitting at the desk with the gooseneck lamp, I was innocent of all of this. The file drawers stuck, and were dusty, and I was covered with dust. I fetched Mr. Shawn's lunch, and tried to be kind to Goldie, the poodle, when she nipped at my legs. Although I had told Mr. Gibbs I had no idea what I wanted to do, by the time a month went by I knew that I wanted to be a writer. I had written no prose whatsoever before, with the exception of school papers. I had written poems, and these began to be published in the magazine, but that in a way is a different story. It strikes me as ludicrous now that I thought Mr. Shawn would be interested in this decision, but I began to try to write "Talk" stories on my own, and to leave them on his desk. I have somewhere, still, the notes he wrote back: *Not for us, quite yet.* Bill and I took a liking to each other and he began to bring me along on assignments, and to teach me how to hold a conversation and a notebook at the same time. I began to bicker more often with the smoke-ring blower, and once, in the middle of one of those arguments, he put the cigarette out in the water rather than on the side of the bathtub and disappeared for days. The *looky-here* was antidote to this. In time I was moved from Mr. Shawn's office and had an office to myself in the Fiction Department, where I read manuscripts all day, and wrote letters on behalf of the editor I worked for who periodically took me out to lunch to cheer me up because I was a nice-looking girl and I was unhappy in love. I was angry at the smoke-blower, from whom I found it impossible to part, and I was secretly in love with a writer at the magazine, who was older than I was, and—of course—married. To me, then, marriage was an inviolate state. That there was ample evidence around me that this wasn't so, exactly—that Mr. Shawn himself, after all, seemed to be conducting two long marriages—confused rather than clarified the issue. These examples had nothing to do with me, or the hazy picture I had of my own future. It did not occur to me to unburden myself to the older writer, or to anyone else, about this. In addition to these romantic longeurs, I was loved by someone else whom through no fault of his, I could not love back. I thought I was the only person on earth ever to be in this predicament. It flattened my spirit.

During that time I thought a great deal about what it meant to be a writer, or, more precisely, what life might have in store for me. I had written poems since I was a small child, almost since I learned how to write, but working as a writer—one who produced "copy," or "pieces"—was new. I knew, vaguely, that it was unlikely that I could support myself writing poems; this is why I had taken a job in the first place. Shortly after I had arrived at the magazine, the kind poetry editor had printed two of my poems, one of which had won a prize at school; this was a long poem, and I correctly surmised that I would never earn as much money from a poem again—I think the total was about twelve hundred dollars. This so far has turned out to be true. The magazine paid ten dollars a line then for poetry; I don't believe this rate has changed. I was then still working on a manual typewriter, an Olympia, and a bell rang when you typed to the end of the line; breaking the line before the bell rang meant a poem, but the ringing bell meant prose, and that meant real money. But I had also begun to love the shape that prose made in my head.

The Fiction Department, housed on the twentieth floor, directly above Mr. Shawn's office, received more than fifty thousand stories a year, and I read a great many of them. Almost all of them were about things that happened, usually suddenly: a car crash, or a death, or unkind words out of nowhere, a door slamming. In my own life at that time, conversely, nothing seemed to happen suddenly: it was more like watching water circle down a drain. There was a tall file cabinet in a sort of foyer outside my office, filled with card files, in alphabetical order. When I read a manuscript, I wrote the name of the author on a card, and recorded, almost always, the day it was returned and whether I had written a personal note. Encouraging notes were sent only to writers who someday might write a story that could conceivably be published, sometime in the future, in the magazine. Sometimes one sentence, glimmering in a mess of prose, would prompt a letter. (As happened more often, this was not the case, and manuscripts received a printed rejection note, from "The Editors.") It was instructive, thumbing through the files, which dated back decades: one Jerome David Salinger, for example, had submitted twenty-eight manuscripts before the magazine had accepted a story called "A Perfect Day for Bananafish." From the notations it was clear that personal notes had been sent after the first five or six submissions. At the bottom of the second and last card was a notation, in fountain pen that had bled a little, that read *see Shawn files.*

One afternoon I happened to be taking a proof down to the

Fact-Checking Department when I ran into Mr. Shawn. I had not seen him for some weeks. I'd been studying my own reflection in one of the oblique mirrors set in the face-powder halls where two walls met at a corner. The presence of these mirrors was explained by Mr. Shawn's attempt to avert encounters with persons he would rather avoid: writers who might ask him, for example, when a piece that the magazine had accepted months ago might run, or for money. Both of these topics were often obscure and difficult, because of Mr. Shawn's reluctance to hurt a writer's feelings or to disclose his own: there were pieces that he accepted that he had no plans ever to run. This was linked to, and complicated by, I believe, his own ever-present feeling of hopefulness and worry, which was in turn tied to a refusal to give in to despair. (This, in turn, was tied to the *we'll get out of this somehow* mentality of "Onward and Upward . . ." and was just one of the ways the magazine bit its own tail.) I think he thought that if a piece just sat long enough, it would transform into something that in some issue *just might work,* that the genius that was somewhere there would announce itself and the editor who was assigned to the piece would eke it out at last and all would be well. This after all was the attitude the magazine (in the person of Mr. Shawn) took to writers who had not produced work in years, because they were blocked, or just couldn't, or in too many instances seemed to attract so very many episodes of personal tragedy or trouble that no sane person could possibly work under these circumstances. It was tacitly understood that for some people mental equilibrium was not in the cards, in the best of times, and that as a whole, people who spend a lot of time waiting for their own Boo Radley to come out will generally find that he will come out. Or they invent him.

Not surprisingly, money played a part. After all, writers were people with families, and apartments and houses and tuition and often ex-wives to support. A person who was beset by these responsibilities needed to be paid. So in a fallow time Mr. Shawn would take a piece that would not run, or in other instances writers on contract were paid a great deal, in those days, for signing that contract, and then had what amounted to a drawing account at the magazine. This meant that there were writers who were so in debt to the magazine, for money which had paid for apartments and tuition and the general high cost of living a certain kind of life in New York, that it became impossible that they would ever pay back the magazine, which was represented in the person of Mr. Shawn. This fostered the—I don't want to say *illusion,* because it had been going on at the time, that is, the early 1980s, when I came to the magazine, for at least twenty years or more—the *notion,* then, of a large extended family in which the Victorian paterfamilias, in his overcoat and muffler, girded against the elements in all weather, was the giver of approval and sustenance. It was written into the contracts of fiction writers that characters who appeared in stories in the magazine could not appear elsewhere for a period of one year. Or was it ten years? Or forever? So that the landscape of the ten-point type became the only air that even the imaginary could breathe.

It was difficult to avoid the mirrors. At first you thought you saw someone down the length of the hall, and then you realized in the same instance in which it occurred you had bumped into yourself. (Later, when I began to write Profiles for the magazine, I often thought of these mirrors.) I was prone to this escapade because I had begun dressing up. By then I wore crocheted dresses over silk slips—the effect was vaguely Guineverish—sold by a woman on Greenwich Avenue, and I liked to catch sight of myself in the mirror. I know now I must have looked faintly ridiculous, like an extra fallen to the cutting floor in a Zeffirelli production. I was wearing one of these getups on this particular afternoon, when I stopped myself from banging my head on the mirror and bumped into Mr. Shawn instead.

It took us both a moment to recover from the jar of physical contact. When we had finished apologizing (Mr. Shawn was under the impression that there was a chance I had been injured, and it took a few moments to dissuade him), he asked me if I was interested in clothes. I had no idea what he might mean by this. I also knew that if Mr. Shawn had asked me if I was interested in bison, or aerodromes, I would develop a sudden and intense interest in these things. I nodded, and he disappeared, as he was prone to do, into the ether. An hour later at my desk I was asked if I could spare a minute to see Mr. Shawn. It was my first private interview, and when I came in he asked me to sit on the only space of the white couch in his office which was free of books and galleys. He told me that the writer who had been writing the column "On and Off the Avenue" had decided, after seven years, she'd like to stop writing it, and he was wondering if it would be possible for me to take it on. This would mean a number of things, he explained. I would need to give up my job in the Fiction

Department, which I might not want to do, but it would be difficult, especially in the fall, for me to do both jobs at once. In order to be sure I understood the kind of writing I was meant to do, he would like me to write a piece of about one thousand words in which I would describe objects for sale in a shop. It could be any shop I liked, in Manhattan. I should of course submit expenses. Most important, he said, he wanted me to think about what I wanted to do, at the magazine. His voice, if possible, dropped to a lower pitch. It was clear to him, he said, that I could be either a writer or an editor, and for now I needed to choose. A writer's life, he said, with a little lift in tone, was, you might say, *unpredictable.*

I was looking down, and I noticed by my feet an enormous pile of manuscripts, about a foot high, that was held together in sections by rubber bands. Since I had placed it there, months ago, I knew, from its particularly smeary feel, that it was some chapters of a novel called *The Runaway Soul,* by a writer called Harold Brodkey, who had been rewriting it for twenty years. When this book was finally published a few years later, there was a party on a balcony of a New York hotel. I was standing in a party frock made out of almost shredded pale silk, and Harold came up to me and gestured to Central Park, which looked that evening as though it were made of fairy lights. He took the drink out of my hand and poured it slowly over the balustrade. Then he said, "You think it will always be like this. Well, it won't." I remember feeling shocked and then sorry that he couldn't be happy at his own party, and also the feeling he was trying to look out for me—in the past months he had often sat on a chair in my office, chatting—and that already I knew he was right. He was dead a few years after that—in the years it seemed that everyone who was brilliant was dead or dying—and a few weeks later I received a note thanking me for writing to him when he was ill, which he had dictated, in his wife's hand.

The next day during my lunch hour I wandered out with a notebook toward Grand Central Station, and the following morning I handed in a story about a shop that specialized in knives. I wrote about carving knives and boning knives and special knives with bone handles for gutting fish. I had another meeting with Mr. Shawn, in which, like a character in a Thornton Wilder play, I told him I had decided to "be a writer." He greeted the news with resignation. He then told me that I had two deadlines, one on October 18 and the other three weeks later, and in each instance I was to write eighteen thousand words. He also mentioned, in tones of embarrassment, that I would be paid a weekly salary throughout the year, rather than for each piece. (I later found out that because I was so young, he was afraid that I would be irresponsible with large sums of money given to me all at once; that this arrangement, when it ended, would have quite the opposite effect, leaving me in an unfortunate position in comparison to that of other writers who were supposedly, by virtue of age, more responsible, was not something he could have predicted.) When I left the office he raised his hand, in a gesture of both valediction and greeting.

I left the Fiction Department, and was given an office on the eighteenth floor, a few steps from the clock. Out of a kind of desperate fear of being found out, I immediately spent three weeks in the magazine's library, among the heavy black bind-

self out the window of his apartment and killed himself. Yet
another. The woman whose mother threatened to blow up her
house and was writing, gradually, a dreamlike book about her
own family's story of murder and incest, left her husband for
another woman, and became a friend without whom I could
not think coherently about my own life. Yet another. I did not
think in the same ways about men's lives because they seemed
remote from my own, with different requirements. Late one
night the telephone rang. It was a friend, the boy who had
chased fire engines, who for what seemed then inexplicable
reasons had been invited to dinner at the apartment of the
woman with whom Mr. Shawn had been living his alternate
life, Goldie's owner. He was calling to tell me that he thought
he was losing his mind: the furnishings of the apartment were
exactly the same as the furnishings of the Shawns' apartment.
He was calling from a pay phone on the corner. Another box.
I began to arrange these files, filling them with what scraps I
could find, swan feathers with tar on them, numbers to call in
an emergency, as if I were filling a curio cabinet, a file chest
like the one in the Fiction Department, filled with stories.

In my office on the eighteenth floor I wrote my columns in
the fall, and short pieces about other things, and stared out the
window at the pigeon on the ledge of the building across the
street. I began to write Profiles. I went to see people in theaters
and on ski slopes and on movie sets, and sat still and listened,
and then asked them questions about their lives. I felt adolescent, still, and covered with scabs. Through all of this I con-
tinued to read the black binders in the library as though my
life depended on it. Because I was shy, and afraid, and set on
not bumping into myself in the mirror, although I did again

and again, I set myself to learn a kind of ventriloquism. The syntax was offhand, precise, it played catch with itself. It told a story without telling a story. It took as given that the story that wasn't told was the important one. When I had worked in the Fiction Department I wrote letters for editors, and one afternoon a letter landed on my desk with the note: *Handle this?* It was a note from Mary McCarthy, complaining that the magazine was not being properly delivered to her address in Paris, where, I knew, she was living with her fourth husband. I wrote back, saying that until she let the magazine know that her subscription was arriving weekly, I would send her the magazine myself from New York, in an airmail envelope. The letter that came back a week later thanked me for taking on this task: the magazine had arrived. She then asked if I was the person, with, she pointed out, the same name, whose poem had been printed in the magazine some weeks ago. She admired the poem, she wanted me to know, but I had made mistakes in my Italian geography. Frankly, she was astonished the Fact-Checking Department had not picked it up. The next week when I sent her the current issue of the magazine, I enclosed a note thanking her for the correction.

During the years I sat thinking and staring out the window on the eighteenth floor, fissures that had long been opening began to tear. At first these seemed like rents in clouds, that would mend themselves. Some of these had to do with facts that were known to everyone, which were never spoken about, but were crucial to the life of the magazine, and enabled its dream life: Mr. Shawn's two households, the knowledge that some persons at the magazine, especially any of the persons who dealt with the world outside the magazine's offices, were invented. The world of the magazine depended on facts; without them, the magazine would float off like a hot air balloon. Facts pinned it down, but *what was real,* after all? Which life did one choose, the one on or off the page? The distinction blurred. The life one talked about, or the life one did not?

The unanswerable was the only answer. It is impossible to know *how it could have turned out,* or *how it might have happened differently:* for in the end, the owners of the magazine decided to sell it. That it was a commercial enterprise, to be bought and sold, had occurred to almost no one, and the web of the magazine as it had existed—with its intact, eccentric inner life—perished. A corollary part of this was that Mr. Shawn was fired. He was seventy-five. A picture of him, finally, appeared in a tabloid paper, getting into a town car on Forty-third Street. He is wearing his overcoat, and his arms are raised, as if wielding off a blow. He looks like a man waking from a dream into a nightmare, or from a nightmare into a dream.

I kept the letter from Mary McCarthy in a file in my drawer, in my tiny apartment with the leaky skylight, marked "important letters." I felt, in a way, an affinity. When I had sat in my office and thought about women's lives she was among the women I thought about. During her marriage to Edmund Wilson, I knew, she had lived briefly in the seaside town where I spent my summers. I knew one of his children a little bit, and had once been to the house near the highway where they had lived. McCarthy had been a friend of my tutor at college. He had introduced me to her, after a lecture, in which she talked about the lawsuit Lillian Hellman had brought against her, after McCarthy had called Hellman a liar, and she said at one point, "Murder is more civilized than divorce. As usual, the Victorians were right." I can't remember what she was referring to—one of her own four marriages? something else?—but I do know I didn't understand, then, what she meant.

After a while the blower of smoke rings went briefly to Montreal, where he knew a girl who would be crueler to him than I could manage to be. A friend of the boy who had chased fire engines was murdered, and the murderer turned out to be someone he knew, and in despair over the end of the magazine and life in general as we imagined it would be, he moved far north, to remote country where at night he listened to hooting owls. I married the man who would be the father of my first child, a painter who spoke in short sentences, and for a little while I dissolved, as people do, into pabulum and mashed banana, and took on the task of showing the world to someone else, whose first sentence was *No wind.* I was, I think now, in a kind of shock. What had it meant to write *for the magazine,* at that time? When I think about that I see the shape of silence, an expanding and contracting cloud, or maybe a kite, in which the right words—and these words were different for each writer, each person for whom the world in a real way was not real unless it was written down—are the knots on the kite string that both lets the kite fly and keeps it tethered to earth. When I was a child my father taught me how to make a kite out of newspaper; a flying machine made of words. When I first came to the magazine, almost everyone at the office or who wrote for the magazine regularly had done so for most of their lives, and I expected to do that, too. That didn't happen.

After the magazine as it had been ended, it took a long time for me to know how to think again. *How ridiculous,* it's almost possible to think now.

Many years later, on a rainy afternoon in Maine, on the Penobscot Peninsula, a friend and I tried to amuse a tribe of little girls by driving from Castine to Blue Hill to get ice cream, and we stopped at an antiques store where the girls could look at old seashells and samplers. (I had driven to Maine from Lake Placid, where I was visiting the family of the son of the man who had written about jazz for the magazine, who had since died; it was long a strangeness in my life that I often knew the parents of my contemporaries before I knew them.) In the corner of the antiques store was a high ormolu chest covered with dust. It was peculiar. There was a double set of drawers running down the front, and a label was fixed to the front of each drawer. In order to pull out the drawers, you needed to release a vertical molding that held the drawers in, by pushing a button. It was, I saw, an elaborate file cabinet. The labels, which were set into rectangular brass plates, were faded but legible. I peered closer to read them. They had been typed on what looked like an old Olympia typewriter. I recognized the font. The labels were in capitals: HARCOURT BRACE, THE NEW YORKER (GENERAL), THE NEW YORKER (SHAWN), PERSONAL, PARIS, LILLIAN HELLMAN, LEGAL (HELLMAN), PERSONAL, PARIS, PRIVATE, CASTINE.

The owner of the shop was nearby, and when I had collected myself, I asked about it. Yes, the chest had belonged to Mary McCarthy. I knew, didn't I, that she had lived in Castine? I did. I had walked over to see what had been her house that morning: a big yellow Federal-style house with a green lawn, a block from the harbor. There was a drawer at the top of the chest with a key in it, and I asked if I could open it. The owner told me to do what I liked, but to be careful—the chest was falling apart. I turned the heavy key and pulled out the drawer. Inside were a score of labels, detailing other categories: SHOP RECEIPTS, WILSON, PARTISAN REVIEW, KNOPF . . .

There were no papers in any of the drawers. I found myself on the edge of tears. The smell of must and a sharp faint smell of something else, verbena or old paper, rose from the chest. The labels "PERSONAL" and "PRIVATE" had been double-typed; the effect was a warning, in bold letters. Those drawers were empty, too.

The girls were ready for ice cream, and we zipped up their slickers against the rain which was really coming down now. The air smelled like wet pine and the girls shrieked, jumping over the puddles. I had just finished a book that I wasn't sure I was going to publish, and I had it with me for my friend to read. When I came back to New York I talked about the chest, and in time, a few days after Christmas, bought for me by my husband, whom I had told about it, it arrived wrapped in old blankets, the key to the drawers still in the locks. For a while it sat in the middle of the dining room, because it distressed me and I did not know what to do with it. It was a time when I was often accused by people around me of compartmentalizing. I found it difficult to answer this, or to figure out how I felt about what was, after all, a gift. Then it was moved upstairs to a room that I had once used as my study, but had become a kind of catchall, between the room's two windows.

Things accumulated on it: a piece of driftwood, a few photographs, a luna moth in a case, some old painted plates, and then more papers, until its power to wound was quelled by disorder, and it became another piece of furniture. I began to stick things in the drawers, willy-nilly. I began to realize that if I thought I had lost something I wanted to keep to myself it was probably in the chest.

Over the few years when I went to lunch with Mr. Shawn at the Algonquin or the Oak Room, at the old Plaza Hotel, where I had crab cakes because I had once ordered them and Mr. Shawn always said, after that, "You like the crab cakes, don't you," and ordered them for me, with a blush of pleasure at remembering. The conversation was the same. I would think of amusing things to tell him beforehand, because I was afraid the conversation would lag, and that silence would rise between us. After a while we would circle around to the same subject. I would mention pieces I might like to write and he would nod. I was then interested in religious communities, a subject about which Mr. Shawn was not particularly keen. I had recently met a woman who lived in a cave. He would then fold his napkin and say, clearing his throat first, "Miss Zarin, have you ever thought of writing fiction?" He believed, he said, I had a fictional turn of mind.

Sometime after that, and after Mr. Shawn had died, I read an account of that same conversation by a woman some years older than I was, and infinitely, to my mind, more glamorous, who had also written for the magazine. I think it occurred at the Oak Room, too. It was, in a way, a comfort. *Gee,* I thought, *really?* I thought about the ticking clock that became a time bomb, and secrets hidden in plain sight, and the black binders in which every word was carefully pasted down. I found myself wondering how often Mr. Shawn saw someone he wanted to talk to, in the mirror. And I thought of the story I had read so long ago, in which the story the characters were reading was the story they had asked for, scribbling themselves into a book that they read aloud to themselves as it happened.

Acknowledgments

The author would like to thank: Deborah Garrison and Peter Matson, Caroline Zancan and her colleagues at Knopf; Holly Brubrach, who as style editor of *The New York Times Magazine* commissioned pieces that became the beginning of this book; Karen Balliett, Sara Barrett, Martin Edmunds, Elizabeth Kramer, Suzannah Lessard, Bill McKibben, Pamela Morton, Jonathan Schell, and Alice Truax, for reading early—and later—versions; Joe, Anna, Rose, Jack, and Beasie, who have given me the best part of the life written about in these pages, and the MacDowell Colony, for two residencies during two winters.

Cynthia Zarin was born in New York City and educated at Harvard and Columbia. The author of four books of poetry and five books for children, she is a longtime contributor to *The New Yorker,* as well as other publications, and a former contributing editor at *Gourmet.* Her awards and honors include a John Simon Guggenheim Fellowship, the Ingram Merrill Award for Poetry, the Peter I. B. Lavan Prize, a National Endowment of the Arts Award for Literature, and the Los Angeles Times Book Prize. She lives in New York City.

A NOTE ON THE TYPE

The text of this book was set in Garamond No. 3. It is not a true copy of any of the designs of Claude Garamond (ca. 1480–1561), but an adaptation of his types, which set the European standard for two centuries. It probably owes as much to the designs of Jean Jannon, a Protestant printer working in Sedan in the early seventeenth century, who had worked with Garamond's romans earlier, in Paris, but who was denied their use because of Catholic censorship. This particular version is based on an adaptation by Morris Fuller Benton.

COMPOSED BY *North Market Street Graphics*
Lancaster, Pennsylvania

PRINTED AND BOUND BY *Berryville Graphics*
Berryville, Virginia

DESIGNED BY *Iris Weinstein*